T0128566

Hanging in the Stars

Pat Gallagher Sassone

authorHOUSE®

AuthorHouse™
1663 Liberty Drive
Bloomington, IN 47403
www.authorhouse.com
Phone: 1-800-839-8640

Published by AuthorHouse 1/25/2012

ISBN: 978-1-4678-5728-4 (sc)
ISBN: 978-1-4678-5727-7 (hc)
ISBN: 978-1-4678-5726-0 (e)

Library of Congress Control Number: 2011960213

This book is printed on acid-free paper.

For my family of storytellers:

my mother, Arlene - the first, funniest, and wisest

my husband, John - generous, intelligent, and witty

our sons, Chris and Tim - rebellious, innovative, and entertaining

CHAPTER 1

Andrew punched the chrome handle to open the glass double doors of the weightroom in the gym. Today, he thought, I'm going to change my skinny little ass. He cautiously eyed the silver machines with the black grips and strange pulleys. Mirrors lined the walls, but Andrew already knew what he'd see there. Sandy hair framing a long, thin face with pale skin that flushed even before his workout had begun. Shoulders up around his ears, knobby elbows bent below the gray T-shirt, bony knees that protruded under baggy red basketball shorts. He jiggled his right foot as he prepared to start his workout.

Quickly he lay down on the mat to begin stretching. As fast as possible he rotated each arm 12 times. Then he alternately raised each knee to his chin. Finally, sitting up, he stretched his arms toward his feet, grabbing at his toes. The backs of his legs were taut.

A big guy with tattooed arms and a wrapped right knee was watching him. Andrew tried to ignore the guy. He eyed the machines and started on the chest press, fumbling to select the right setting for the seat. Somehow he caught his thumb in the spring. He squinted to read the directions on the side of the machine. First he placed his hands inside the grip, and then he tried the palms outside. He moved the pin several times in an effort to find the correct weight. Slowly he pushed the weights forward.

After three sets of eight repetitions he moved to the next station. Free weights using dumbbells for overhead presses. He sat there with his legs bent for support and a dumbbell in each hand. He lifted his right arm straight up and down. The left was almost all the way up when he dropped the dumbbell.

"Oh shit," he called.

"Shit, that's for sure," replied the big guy.

Andrew knew his name, Cruz. He was a biker who had wrecked his knee, but not his Harley, in a recent accident. All the kids in the neighborhood knew that.

"Listen kid, I saw you pretending to work out."

Andrew sat speechless while the red climbed up his neck. He didn't want to stare at Cruz's enormous biceps, or his snake tattoo. It looked like a cobra.

"Want some help, Blushing Beauty?"

"Yeah," Andrew blurted. "I'd really like that." Andrew wondered what was coming next.

"Okay, I'll help you get in shape, but everything has its price. You know my sister, Maya? She's in school with you. She's got the killer shot on the handball court at the park."

"Yeah," Andrew replied, wondering what was coming next.

"According to her, you are some kind of brainiac. I want you to help my sister learn to read better. Read and nothing else. You understand?"

"Me? You're going to help me work out, and I'm supposed to help your sister read?"

"She's having trouble in English class with that Shakespeare shit."

"Yeah, okay. I just got to make sure I can. I'll get back to you."

Andrew was so unnerved by Cruz talking to him that he just wanted to run as far away as he could. He leapt off the bench, ran out of the gym, and hopped on his bike.

Riding home, he tried to figure out what just happened. He thought, Weird, really weird, that motorcycle guy, Cruz, coming up to me like that. Cruz is definitely scary, but his Harley is mad cool. What I wouldn't do to ride that. Yeah, fat chance that's going to happen. I'm not even sure if I can build biceps in my arms, no less help Maya read.

Bursting to tell someone about his encounter with Cruz, Andrew rode to Max Donner's house. He went an extra block to avoid the Mustang cruising the avenue--Cruz's boys looking for trouble. Whenever the car passed him, Andrew could feel those guys laughing at him pedaling his dumb bike.

The avenue was a street filled with storefronts: the pizzeria, OTB, bars, a laundromat, a bowling ally, a bank, and a drugstore. The Ave. served as a dividing line between modest middle-class ranch and split-level family homes like Andrew's on the north side, and the attached houses and old, decrepit apartment buildings on the south side.

Andrew relaxed as he turned off the avenue and headed north toward home. Since Labor Day the sound of kids playing on the streets and the smell of barbeque cooking had diminished. Though it was still pretty warm outside, a back –to-school feel was in the air. This week Andrew was happy to have started high school. Pretty soon the cold weather would drive everyone except the dog walkers indoors.

Andrew had lived in this neighborhood all his life. As a little kid, he liked growing up here in Queens. The neighborhood had a city feel, with stores, lights, and an energetic vibe, yet the blocks were tree-lined and families had backyards and space enough so that kids could play sports or hang out. But lately he was thinking what it would be like to live somewhere completely different, like New Zealand. Of course, if he moved to New Zealand, he couldn't crash in Max's basement whenever he needed an escape from his mom.

He always felt happy turning into Max's driveway. For as long as Andrew could remember, Max had been his best friend. Living around the corner from each other, all they had to do was hop their back fence to hang out together. "Anybody home?" Andrew called, opening the Donners' side door.

"Andrew! So how is high school treating my other son?" asked Max's mother. "I hear you two aren't in any classes together this year. What happened?"

"I don't know, Mrs. Donner. Blame the computer gods."

"I'm down here," Max yelled from his basement.

"Who is serving you now, Master Max? X-Box, Nintendo, Wii?" Andrew called as he went down the basement stairs.

"He's going to marry an avatar someday," shouted Max's mother. "You will be the best man."

"Ma give us some space. So what's up, Andrew? Let me see your program card." Andrew handed it over. Max looked disgusted at the names of Andrew's ninth grade teachers.

"Yeah, we have a lot of the same teachers, a mix of bores and workaholics, right?" Andrew said. "Except for Sikorski, I have him for English class ninth period. He seems cool."

"I have him first period," said Max.

"Did he tell your class about that club he runs called Notes? Something to do with writing music and lyrics using computers. It meets on Wednesday afternoons. Sounds kind of fun."

He was sure Max would agree. Max lived for computers and always talked about writing for a band. But he just said, "We'll see."

"Okay," Andrew agreed. "Hey, you'll never guess who started talking to me at the gym?"

"My mom."

"Very funny. You know that guy Cruz with a bull's body? He rides a Harley."

"Yeah, what did he want you to be leader of the pack? All 100 pounds of you."

"No, we talked about working out. His sister plays handball in the park. You want to take a ride over there? I could get into handball."

"What's the chance those kids carrying box cutters will play with us?" Max asked, looking down at the phone screen on his lap.

Andrew realized he couldn't tell Max about Cruz, not today or ever. He and Max had a long history of fun together. Last year in music class, Max's arm farts synchronized with John Philip Sousa's marches made Andrew laugh long into the summer. But Max didn't like shaking things up. He never wanted to leave the block.

"Are you staying for dinner, Andrew?" Mrs. Donner called. He could hear the clang of silverware and smell the tempting aroma of garlic and peppers and onions.

"No, my mom gets all bent out of shape if I don't tell her changes of schedule in advance. Thanks anyway."

From the corner of Max's block Andrew could see his mother getting out of her black Honda, carrying groceries and dry cleaning while checking her Blackberry.

"Hey, Mom," he called.

"Andrew, I 'm so glad you're here to help. I'm running late. Get a gallon of water from the garage. Ally has to be at practice by 6:30."

When he opened the garage door, Ally elbowed him out of the way. "I got it. Move out of the way, bro," his sister Ally said as she stretched her long legs over him to grab the container.

"That's some black and blue you got on your shin," he said to his sister. "Ever heard of shin guards?"

"You should see the other team's fullback," Ally said. She raised both hands up in a victory sign while gently shaking her head to move her long, dark red hair out of her eyes.

"I bet," Andrew answered. He put his bike away and locked it.

That bruise was a sure sign of a hustler for the college coaches who would be evaluating Allyson's ability on the soccer field at a showcase game. Maybe black and blue with rainbow background would qualify her for a full college scholarship.

In the dining room he could hear his mother's deep, clear voice talking about some employee in her office.

"I told him in no uncertain terms I wasn't about to put up with those kind of comments. You know how men are," his mom said to Ally.

His mother often made negative comments about men. Andrew wanted to ask her, Well, just how are men? How would you know, since Dad ran out on you ten years ago?

Andrew didn't really remember the divorce that well. At first, his dad did try to stay involved in Ally's and his life. He rented an apartment nearby so he could visit on Sundays. He would take them to the movies or a ballgame or bowling. It was fun. During winter break the three of them went to a ski resort and to the beach in the summer. One vacation their Dad took Ally and him to Disney World.

But his mom always found faults with the visits. His dad was giving them too much sugar to eat, or he let them watch too much violence on TV, or got them home way past their bedtime. Then, two years ago, his dad remarried and moved out of the city, about an hour's drive from Andrew's house. His new wife was nice, but this year they had a baby boy and much less time to visit. This year his dad only saw Ally and him on holidays.

His mother was relieved that she didn't have to deal with their dad on a regular basis. She was a no-nonsense bank manager who ran her home in pretty much the same way she ran the bank. Her direct toughness was hard enough. But she annoyed Andrew even more when she tried to be diplomatic.

Tonight at dinner she again casually suggested, "Andrew have you thought about trying out for track? You look like a runner."

Why not blurt it right out? thought Andrew. With your skinny little ass you might as well be the water boy. A couple of nights before, she'd suggested he might try out for drama club.

"All my girlfriends thought you were so cute in the school play last year," Ally added.

Cute? 5 feet 4, 120 pound guy? Cute? How pathetic, thought

Andrew. His sister's friends were boring too. Allyson's friends texted each other 100 times a day about boys and clothes. They spent every day worrying about getting in some college. They joined as many activities as possible to enhance their college applications. Like Ally thinking soccer was her ticket to some hot-shot school. Ally and her friends were so predictable.

Maya, Cruz's sister, wouldn't be caught dead staying after school in some club. Andrew knew that Maya cut classes to hang out with the guys on the handball court. He had seen her playing handball. Her tight body sliding sideways. She was probably stronger than him. But she sure was pretty with that long black hair that kind of swayed as she moved.

Last year, when he was in eighth grade, everything was different. Now the last thing he wanted to do was be on a dumb school team like Allyson's or act with those weirdoes in drama. Sometimes he felt like screaming at his mother: I might want to be a graffiti artist and paint curse words all over every school in the city. Maybe I'll become a street performer, a juggler in the park. No overhead, no college degree, no business suit. That sounds like a plan I can follow.

"Remember, Andrew, today is the fifteenth of the month. It's your turn to clear the table. Don't forget to sweep the floor and wipe the counters. One thing I can't stand is a sticky counter."

He dreaded the schedule his mother would come up with next year when Ally started college. How would his mother cope when Ally finally went away to college? So much of her time and energy went into making Allyson the star student athlete on her way to conquering the male-dominated world.

Andrew wanted to fight back. Yeah, I'll do it, he thought. I'll work out with Cruz and help Maya in English. But how would he and Cruz set up a plan for the workouts and tutoring sessions? He'd have to make the arrangements quickly, before Cruz got someone else to help Maya. In the evenings, he'd seen Cruz on the Ave. bowling or playing pool in the local bar, The Pit. If he went over there, he'd have a good chance of finding Cruz.

How to get out from under his mother's watchful eye? Gradually he introduced school into the dinner conversation, saying he was reading *Romeo and Juliet* in English class. His mother was immediately enthusiastic.

"Oh, *Romeo and Juliet,* I read that in high school. Ally, did you have the same English teacher as Andrew in ninth grade? I remember you doing some creative assignments in that class."

"I had Sikorski too. I loved *Romeo and Juliet.*"

Andrew just rolled his eyes as his mother and Ally got sappy over this play. But now he could invent a reason for leaving the house.

"Well, I have to make a sword for the fight in the opening scene. We're acting it out. I have to get some poster board and glue."

"Oh, we did that too," Ally said.

Andrew nodded. He didn't mention that the sword was optional.

"When is this due? Wait, let me guess. Tomorrow," his mother said.

"You guessed it, Mom. I'll be right back. I'll just ride over to Kim's Stationery. They'll have what I need."

"Maybe you can get a planner while you're there. So we don't have to go through this last- minute nonsense."

"I have a planner, Mom. Remember, you gave it to me in July?" Andrew said, slipping out the front door. He could feel his mother's frustration in her silence.

The avenue was crowded with commuters coming home from work in the city. As Andrew had expected, the red Mustang was parked directly behind the back door of The Pit. He walked over and peeked in through the rear window. He could hear the crack of the wooden pool sticks and the clang of glass beer bottles. Cruz's posse was in the middle of a game.

Suddenly the back door opened. Ray, one of Cruz's guys, yelled, "Do you see any bike racks here?" He grabbed Andrew by the front of his sweatshirt. "What do you want, hairball?"

Before Andrew could answer, out stepped Cruz. "Easy does it with Blushing Beauty. How about calling you BB for short? We don't want nothing to happen to BB's brain until he teaches Maya to speak Shakespeare. So what do you say, BB, we got a deal?"

Andrew nodded, afraid to speak. Behind Cruz, Ray seethed, smoking nonstop.

"A man of few words is a smart man indeed," said Cruz. "Meet me tomorrow morning at 7 AM sharp at the gym. I'll show you the workout--Cruz's insider tips. Those muscles are gonna rip that shirt in two." Then he laughed, a loud, crazy laugh.

"After school you'll meet Maya at the swings near the handball court for her first lesson. If she's not there tomorrow, I want to know right away. *Comprendo?*"

"*Si,* yes, okay," Andrew said, getting on his bike with Cruz still laughing at him. Andrew wasn't sure if that was good or bad. He was so excited from his meeting with Cruz that he rode halfway home before he realized he forgot the materials he needed to make the sword. Riding back past The Pit, he could hear Cruz yelling inside the bar.

The next morning Andrew got up before six. Cruz had said, "7 AM sharp."

His mother definitely would not want him to associate with people like Cruz and Maya. He waited until his mom was in her office mode, leaving for work. Then he said, "Mom, I've been thinking about how you said I should consider running track. So I plan on hitting the gym a few mornings before school and running in the park after school. I need to get in shape for the team."

"Well, Andrew, that sounds great as long as it doesn't interfere with schoolwork.

Make sure that you're out of the gym, showered, and on time to your first period."

"Mom, remember this year I'm on late session. My first period doesn't start until 9:05."

"Okay, then. How did that sword turn out?"

"Unbelievable. All the Montagues and Capulets will cower when I draw my cardboard dagger."

"Don't be sarcastic, Andrew. It doesn't suit you. Have a good day. Make sure to check the fridge for your list of chores. We want to get into the school schedule as quickly as possible. Remind Ally to check the list too if you see her before you leave for the gym."

"Sure, Mom," he said. But Andrew was already focusing on his upcoming meeting with Cruz. He rode as quickly as he could to the gym. When he entered the weight room, Cruz looked up at the clock. Cruz, with a barrel chest and huge biceps, was lifting a barbell with two huge 45- pound plates on each end. Sweating like a mule, he heaved and lifted. He grabbed the weights like he grabbed at life. As soon as he finished the set, Cruz waved for Andrew to join him.

"Come on, come on. Move it. Let me show you the workout." He got up and grabbed a chart lying underneath the bench. Sitting next to Andrew, Cruz laid out the chart, where he had meticulously sketched out a series of cardio and weight training exercises. The sketches were very detailed, and the instructions on how to do each exercise were clear and complete. Then, with near-perfect form, Cruz demonstrated each exercise. Andrew thought Cruz was better than any of his gym teachers. But he wondered what miracle it would take for him to get in that kind of shape.

Cruz explained, "We'll meet once a week, say every Wednesday. Then I'll check your progress. But you gotta bust your ass at least three days a week, or I'm gonna bust it for you," his voice bellowed. Good thing the room was pretty empty.

"Okay, thanks, I'll start tomorrow."

"You'll start now. Don't try any shortcuts. I can always tell," Cruz said as he strutted out, leaving Andrew alone.

Andrew moved awkwardly from machine to machine, trying to follow Cruz's instructions. There were at least a dozen machines plus benches with free weights. They seemed to be arranged for the upper body, then legs and your core, like the ab cruncher. There were a lot of mats and different size colored balls too. By the time Andrew left the gym, he felt as if he'd had an outer body experience.

He tried to hustle to school, but he was still fifteen minutes late to his first period class. Luckily, the social studies teacher, Ms. Pearlmutter, was so busy trying to get the smart board to display a time line, she didn't seem to notice him slip into his seat. Concentrating on schoolwork in any class seemed impossible. He kept thinking about Cruz lifting that bar bell and his personal workout chart, which Andrew looked at countless times during the day. Cruz drew the diagrams so well.

But he knew he had to pay attention in English, because his first tutoring session with Maya was this afternoon. He felt really dumb carrying that cardboard sword in the hallway to English class. When he got there, all the desks had been pushed back. Ski told them to get ready to perform the opening scene of *Romeo and Juliet*. The scene involved sword fights between the Montagues and Capulets and the citizens of Verona. The fight escalated from the servants to the lords.

Kids crowded around Ski's desk, which was covered with toy swords, some Star Wars light sabers, and a few cheesy little plastic swords that were left over from Halloween. One student had even brought his grandfather's jeweled sword from India, which Ski had to lock in the principal's closet.

When Ski called out, "Losers, listen up," the class laughed and quieted down immediately. Andrew knew most teachers couldn't pull this off. Kids out of their seats cooperating easily with the teacher. But Ski communicated well with them. He knew how to make them laugh. He wore jeans and a plaid shirt, but the lines around his sky-blue eyes and the gray in his brownish hair showed his middle age. Andrew had heard he drank quite a bit, although no one ever saw him the least bit drunk near school.

In the beginning of the scene a servant of the Capulets bites his thumb at a servant of the Montagues. Neal Peppitone, one of the students who was sitting on the window sill, yelled out, "He gave him the finger. I'd fight him too." Andrew waited on the sidelines for his cue, when the citizens of Verona rush in to duel. Here Andrew yelled out his only line, "Clubs, bills and partisans! Strike! Beat them down. Down with the Capulets! Down with the Montagues!"

Then Andrew lunged at Sally Wareham, who was playing one of the Capulet servants. She immediately fell to the floor, moaning in pain. For some crazy reason the dead and the wounded seem to be having more fun on the classroom floor. Within a few minutes everyone, even the dead, was moaning on the floor. Andrew had so much fun he almost forgot about his meeting with Maya—but not quite. It was always there, like a question mark at the end of the day.

CHAPTER 2

After school he headed to the park. Andrew really liked this spot. It was a big area divided into smaller sections. There was a band shell and a grassy area with barbeque pits and wooden tables for families to picnic. Andrew often played on the softball field and basketball court. A tougher group of kids hung out in the area near the handball court next to the playground.

When he walked by the cyclone fence surrounding the playground, he saw her sitting on a swing, thumbs moving along her phone pad. His throat tightened. Maya kind of scared him. How disgusting - afraid of a girl. The truth was Maya wasn't the only girl who scared him.

Obviously she wasn't afraid of him. As soon as she looked up, she started waving wildly, "*Hola*, Andrew!" When he sat on the swing beside her, he felt jittery. Dressed in her skinny jeans and denim jacket, she looked hot.

Laughing, she asked, "Where's your sword? Did your class have that sword fight too?"

" Yeah, pretty crazy. Since my sword was made from cardboard and aluminum foil at 9 o'clock last night, I donated it to Ski's pile of weapons."

"I like to keep my weapon with me," she said. Ever so slightly she opened her denim jacket pocket to show him a small switchblade.

Andrew tried to stay cool. But he thought, Not bad enough

I'm afraid of fighting her brother. Now I have to worry about protecting myself from her too?

On the courts, next to the swings, several games of handball were going on. The sound of the ball hit relentlessly against the wall echoed throughout the park. The players, mostly guys, many of them shirtless, smashed the ball against the wall. The idea was to hit it low and hard so the other guy couldn't return it. He knew that Maya had one of the best killer shots in the park. Some of the guys refused to play with her.

"What do you think of the play so far?" Andrew asked.

"Sikorski says it's written in English, but I don't know nobody who talks like that."

"Yeah, I hear you," Andrew said. "Let's do the homework and see if we can figure it out."

They sat side by side on the swings, her little notebook open on her tight thigh. Her small brown hands with delicate fingers ending in purple nails held a broken pencil. She didn't bring her book with her, so they shared. Andrew liked when she leaned in next to him. She smelled like peppermint, clean and light.

Andrew read the first question, "Why do the servants start fighting?"

Maya said, "They are some kind of miners who will not carry coals."

Laughing, Andrew said, "Not exactly. Do you see the notes on the opposite page of the play? They explain Shakespeare's language. The first note tells you in Shakespeare's time the word *coals* meant insults."

She rolled her eyes, laughed, and said, "No way. I have to read those notes, plus the play? That's way too much. I won't do it."

"Well, then you won't understand the play."

"Sure I will, because I have you to explain it to me."

"Explain it and do the work for you are two different things."

"Okay, okay, I'll read a note or two. So let me get this straight. The servants start fighting because of insults, right?"

Andrew nodded.

Maya continued, "I know all about that. Same as today. Respect is everything on the street. That's the way it is and has always been."

As they continued to answer the homework questions, Andrew could see Maya got bored quickly. When a question asked to describe the setting of *Romeo and Juliet*, Maya took Andrew's marker and drew a boot of Italy on his loose leaf binder. Inside the boot in aqua ink she wrote, "Verona," the city where *Romeo and Juliet* takes place.

"What are you doing? That's my new binder," Andrew complained.

"It's hotter with Maya's Italian boot on the cover."

When listing the characters in the play, she insisted on writing all the Montagues names on Andrew's hands and the Capulets on her hands.

"Maya, how are you going to hand in this homework tomorrow?"

" 'Palm to palm is holy palmers' kiss.' That's what the play says right here. We won't wash our hands until Ski checks them."

"You're crazy!"

"Definitely, and you are a cutie."

After that, Andrew insisted that she write down the answers on loose leaf. She continually said, "This is so boring," as she printed the answers. Often Andrew had to double-check his answers by looking back at the play. Maya said, "This is taking way too long. I thought you knew the answers."

Andrew knew he needed to make this more fun. He thought she would like the dialogue better if he read it aloud. Though he was embarrassed, Andrew read a line from the play that Ski had used to explained the importance of sound of the words. Andrew read aloud. "How silver sweet sound lover's tongues by night." He thought that Maya would make fun of him. But instead, she replied, "Awesome."

When they finished the last homework question, she shouted, "*Gracias*, Brainiac."

Out of nowhere she hugged him. He could feel his face flush; she said, "You're adorable."

Quickly she stuck the little notebook in her back pocket. Andrew couldn't help but admire that cute butt. Andrew suggested they meet on Friday at the library, because writing answers while sitting on a swing wasn't easy.

Maya said, "No way. I like to keep my eye on the handball court."

"We'll meet here unless it rains." Just then, the Mustang pulled up to the gate.

"*Adios*," she shouted as she ran to the car and got into the back seat. Ray was sitting shotgun next to Cruz. From where he stood, Andrew could see Cruz sitting in the front. Suddenly he turned around and slapped Maya across the face.

That night, Andrew lay awake in his room for a long time, worrying about Maya.

Should he call her? They had exchanged phone numbers at the park. Why did her brother slap her like that? Was it something to do with him? Maybe the hug. Cruz had told him in the gym, hands off his sister. But, she had hugged him. Where was Maya now? Was she safe? He couldn't imagine the humiliation of being slapped across the face.

The next day he waited for her outside her English class. She wasn't there. When he asked one of the kids in the class about her, the classmate said, "Ah, she's hardly ever in class."

Andrew sent her a text: R U OK?

Instantly his phone beeped. Meet me at the swings in the park at 7 pm tonight.

Without hesitating he typed-- See u at 7.

Getting past his mother on Friday night was surprisingly easy. Most Fridays he played computer games at Max's house around the corner. So when he said he was going out, his mom gave the usual curfew, "Be home by 10."

As he walked toward the park, Max texted him: Where r u? Panini getting cold. Had to eat yours. Delicious!

Quickly Andrew replied: Had to go to Ally's practice tonight. See u tomorrow.

About two blocks from the park, Andrew heard the Mustang screeching as it suddenly pulled in alongside the curb next to him. Maya hung out of the window, screaming, "Get in, Andrew. Get in." His heart racing, he looked inside the car for Cruz.

Steely, Cruz's wing man, drove. With dirty blond hair slicked back, a scarred face and huge shoulders, he didn't need much more to make him look scary. As usual, Ray, in a wife beater shirt, sat shotgun. When Andrew climbed in next to Maya, Ray sneered, "No bike tonight? Hope you don't have a flat, Junior."

"His name is Andrew. He's my *amigo*, so be nice to him," shouted Maya, slapping Ray in the back of the head.

"Just *amigos*? Are you really sure, Maya?" asked Ray. "Just in case your brother wants to know."

"Shut up, Ray. You make my head hurt," said a voluptuous girl who was putting on makeup in the back seat next to Maya.

Maya moved to make room for Andrew. Instantly Andrew could smell the sweet aroma of weed. He had never smoked, but he recognized the smell from the stairwell in the school basement. Andrew couldn't believe he was sitting inside the cherry-red Mustang with the gold rimmed tires. He sank into the soft beige leather. Maya cuddled up against his chest while the amplified sound of rock surrounded them.

"Cool car," Andrew commented. "Is it your brother's?"

"Actually it's mine," Steely answered. "A gift from Maya's brother. Since we use it for business, it could be a substantial tax write off, if we paid taxes." Then he started laughing loudly. The Mustang sped down the road with the wind whipping their faces. Without any warning Steely turned and pulled to a tall grassy spot near the bridge.

"Party time," shouted the girl.

Ray popped open the tops of a couple of beers inside a brown paper bag.

"Corona okay, Junior?"

"His name is Andrew," Maya insisted.

"What's in a name?" whispered Andrew in Maya's ear.

"What is it Cruz calls him? Blushing Beauty, BB for short. Are you blushing now, BB?"

Andrew felt his face flush, but he said nothing. The busty girl passed the weed to Andrew, who quickly handed it to Steely. Andrew gulped the beer as they sat and listened to the music. A warm feeling rushed around his stomach and made his head light.

"Time for me and Bianca to have some private time. Everybody out of the car," screamed Steely.

Andrew couldn't wait to get out. Feeling lightheaded from the beer, he easily took Maya's hand in his. He whispered, "I've been so worried about you. I saw your brother slap you. Why'd he do that?"

"My brother doesn't play. He is very strict. The dean called about my cutting classes. My brother went crazy. Like he didn't drop out of school."

"Your brother shouldn't have hit you, but he's right about you not cutting classes."

"I have to cut classes."

"Why?"

"To play handball. My brother makes me come straight home from school. He doesn't want me on the streets. He's afraid of what will happen to me, what I will become."

"Your brother is afraid you'll get hurt," Andrew said.

"If anyone hurt me, he would kill them. I know that. It's more than me getting hurt. It's about him controlling me. So I have to go school, come right home, do homework, cook and clean like my grandmother. Well, I have news for him, I won't live like that. I need a life too. I don't care if I have to fight him."

"What does your grandmother say?"

"She's afraid of him too. Every night she yells at me, "Hurry, get the food on the table. Your brother will be home soon. He will be hungry." I tell her, "This is America; let him get his own food. You're the grandmother, you should be in charge, not him. But she won't listen."

"The women in my family have no problem being in charge. That's for sure," said Andrew.

"That's the way women are today," Maya said. "My brother is living in the past. Tonight at dinner we're talking about the weekend, my brother demands I go to church with my grandmother on Sunday. I said nothing, but I thought, When was the last time you were in church? A lot of good church did him. Let him beat me, I don't care. If I have to run away, I will."

Andrew didn't know what to say. So he just held her hand tighter, and she squeezed his hand in reply. They walked along a little path through the grass and looked up at the stars.

She asked, "Do you like the stars, Andrew?"

"Yeah, a lot. Every summer Max's family takes me camping with them. The coolest things are the stars. Because it's dark in the country, you can see stars everywhere, like a billion diamonds in the night."

"Did you know stars shine in the daytime? The only reason we can't see them is the sun. My sixth-grade teacher taught me that. Isn't that cool?"

"Very. Even now with the street lights, we can see some," said Andrew, looking up to the sky.

"Pick one, Andrew. Choose your star and wish. Ready?"

Andrew nodded.

"Ready, set, wish!" shouted Maya.

Andrew wished on a star that Cruz wouldn't hit Maya again.

After he wished, Andrew turned and kissed her.

It was the first time Andrew had really kissed a girl. Maya's lips had felt so soft. Though the kiss was over in seconds, the warm feeling deep inside Andrew lingered. He had never felt anything quite as wonderful as this. They sat quietly holding hands until

Steely blared the horn and shouted, "Get your asses back in this car pronto, or find out how long the walk home really is."

On the drive home Ray passed around more beer. Not to look like a wimp, Andrew kept taking gulps. He was starting to feel sick.

When Maya went to take a slug, Steely said, "Don't even think about it. Tonight your brother only let you out because I'm watching. Bad enough we picked up BB here. I don't need no heat from your brother over you drinking or smoking."

Maya made an awful face at him and mumbled something in Spanish, Steely said, "I heard that, and you know what your brother will do if he hears about it."

At the Ave. Steely pulled over. "BB, this is your stop. I wouldn't go to The Pit for one last beer if I was you. You don't look too cool." Then he laughed and Ray laughed louder, sticking his head out the window and pointing at Andrew as the car peeled down the Ave.

On Friday night, groups of kids hung out on practically every street corner, many of them high, waiting for some action. Andrew knew in this condition he could easily be jumped if he came across the wrong people. He only had to go a few blocks. He kept telling himself he wasn't going to throw up. But every step he took, he felt worse. Then he noticed the cop car riding slowly next to him. Ally's best friend, Carolyn's father was a cop. He definitely didn't want to meet him here in this shape.

The cop driving the car was young. He called out to Andrew, "Young man, do you need assistance?"

"No, officer, I'm fine."

He thought how his mother would freak out if he was brought home drunk by the cops. The police car was pulling over.

Andrew tried waving him on. "I'm okay, really."

Then miraculously, a call came over the radio. The cop said, "Go home. Get off the Avenue" and sped away.

Relieved, Andrew thought, if I can just make it to the corner, I'll throw up in that trash can. But he couldn't take another step.

Right there, in the middle of the sidewalk with cars driving by, Andrew vomited. He heard some girls coming out of the diner nearby yelling, "How disgusting."

Actually, after puking, he felt better. He could see the lights on in his dining room. Barely able to walk straight and stinking like vomit--how was he ever going to make it past his mother? He fumbled getting the key in the lock. He could hear the sound of the kettle whistling. His mother was in the kitchen making a cup of tea.

"Is that you, Andrew?

"Yeah, Mom."

"Do you want something to eat? I just made yogurt and raisin bars."

The mention of food made him sick.

"No, mom, I'm beat. I'm going to take a shower and go right to bed. See you tomorrow."

He barely made it into the bathroom, where he threw up again. He tried to clean up as well as he could. Tomorrow he would get up early and scrub everything. Good thing his mother had her own bathroom off her bedroom.

He stood under the shower to wash away the smell. He could barely get into clean clothes and hide the dirty ones in the back of his closet. Tomorrow he would toss them.

As he lay in his bed the room spun around him. The last thing he heard was his mother calling from the bottom of the stairs: "Andrew?"

In the middle of the night he heard Ally in the bathroom yelling, "O God, it stinks in here." He could hear her scrubbing and spraying disinfectant. Then he went back to sleep.

CHAPTER 3

When he woke up late the next morning, his head was killing him. On the kitchen fridge, Andrew looked in disgust at the list of things to do that his mother had left for him before she went to work. Thank God the bank was open on Saturday mornings.

Ally was at the counter shoveling yogurt into her mouth. She said, "On my way to practice last night with Carolyn, we drove by the park, and you'll never guess who I saw getting into a car? Especially since, what did you tell mom? Something about playing computer games with Max."

"Back off," Andrew snarled. "So what if I did see some friends?"

"What did you do in the park? The bathroom smelled like a sewer when I got home. I cleaned it. Maybe I should have let mom in on your stinking secret Friday night outing. Listen up, little bro. Obviously you had no trouble finding and drinking lots of beer. The legal age for drinking alcohol is twenty-one. You're fourteen. Do the math. And the park, especially on Friday nights, is infested with drugs. Nothing but trouble. You should stay far away."

"Yeah, and how would you know? What kind of trouble have you ever gotten in on Friday nights? Oh yeah, I remember, you got locked in the library."

Ally shot him a warning look. "Just don't do anything stupid."

"No I wouldn't want to make you look bad. What would your yearbook say? Scholar athlete, sister of a badass?"

Ally really got on his nerves. Wasn't his mother's micromanagement bad enough? He looked at his mother's list again to see if she wanted him to iron his jock strap, and then he crumbled the list and stuffed it the trash can.

Somehow he made it through the weekend without his mother finding out about Friday night. On his way to school on Monday, he stopped by the gym. Cruz was usually there in the morning. Getting in shape was now Andrew's priority. He didn't even care if he was late for first period. Cruz was already in the middle of his workout. It seemed as if he had every plate in the gym stacked on the leg press, and his quads bulged as he did rep after rep. His biceps weren't the only muscles that were huge and strong.

"Yo, if it isn't BB? Heard you had quite a party Friday in the back seat with my sister. That will destroy your workout for sure. Well let's see if you know how to do the basic exercises."

Cruz watched Andrew go through each exercise. "Have you taught my sister to speak Shakespeare yet?"

"She's pretty smart."

"Yeah, keep looking at her brain." His big, broad face was moving in close to Andrew's when Cruz's phone went off. As Cruz turned his back and moved toward the locker, Andrew couldn't help notice Cruz's i Phone and the expensive sneakers.

"How many kilos are we talking about?" mumbled Cruz."Don't ever tell me you don't got the money." He grabbed his jacket and left.

Andrew thought Cruz was exciting--the way he glided in and out of the gym. Those big muscular hands. On the street Cruz's skull ring glimmering, while he revved up the Harley. His muscular chest covered in a leather jacket. His raw, loud laugh echoing in the streets. In the gym Andrew could see guys were looking at him, probably because he'd talked to Cruz. It felt good.

That afternoon when Andrew went to the park, he saw

Maya hanging upside down from the bar where the swings were attached.

"What are you doing, loco girl?"

"I'm hanging in the stars. Don't you remember they're all around us? See, I'm doing my homework. You should be proud of me, Brainiac."

Their homework question was to discuss Romeo's quote, "I fear too early, for my mind misgives some consequence yet hanging in the stars."

The quote reminded Andrew of one of his mother's favorite sayings, "Actions have consequences." Somehow she only said it when the consequences were painful. He tried to put it out of his mind.

Rereading the quote, Andrew explained, "In this scene, Maya, Romeo is on his way to a Capulet party, and he's worried because 'the consequences are hanging in the stars.' He is upset that something bad is going to happen if he parties with his enemies."

Maya answered, "Whatever, in this play the stars somehow predict your future. I guess that's why we're still wishing on them. I like that wishing part a lot. Today in class Ski asked me if I had control over my future or if luck controlled what happened to me."

"What did you say?"

"*Nada*, I don't answer in class. It's not my style. Anyway, my brother controls my future."

Andrew stared at her. "That's not true, Maya. Maybe now, but not always."

Maya seemed unsure, but she squeezed Andrew's hand as she had done the night before. He squeezed back and whispered, "And palm to palm is holy palmers' kiss,"

"So what does that mean, Brainiac?"

"For religious pilgrims traveling to holy places in Shakespeare's times touching hands was like kissing."

"Do you think if my brother saw us holding hands, he would care about holy palmers?"

"Is your brother at the park now?"

"What if he is, I'm never supposed to hold a guy's hand. Now that we are palm to palm, let's wish on a star like we did Friday night."

"Let me get this straight. It's daytime, so we're wishing on the stars that are here but we just can't see," said Andrew.

"That makes it more fun."

Looking up at the sunny sky, Andrew thought, Holding hands isn't all that the churchgoers in Shakespeare's time made it out to be. So he wished on the invisible stars, "Let me not be afraid to kiss Maya." No sooner had he wished it than he turned, and she kissed him on the lips.

He put his arms around her slim waist and kissed her soft lips again. Her kisses made him feel so warm inside. He wanted to keep kissing her again and again. He knew he had to stop now. She felt so soft, he knew he had to leave. He could never find the right words to explain this to Maya. Without an explanation, he blurted out, "I better go."

"See you *manana*," she replied.

Walking toward the bike rack, he felt as if he and Maya were living in a special, secret world. He thought, No wonder guys lose their minds over girls. When Andrew knelt down to unlock his bike from the rack, he was choked from behind and thrown to the ground. Within seconds Ray was on top of his chest, holding a knife to his throat. Standing behind him, smirking, were two other guys, Dexter and Rolly from Cruz's posse. Andrew couldn't breathe and was afraid if he moved Ray would cut his throat.

Ray sneered, saying, "Junior, if you're so smart, you would know helping Maya with her homework doesn't involve kissing her. I'm watching you. We're all watching." He was moving the knife up toward Andrew's nose when he heard Maya screaming,

"Let him go. I'm gonna kill you, Ray." Maya had her knife out.

"Oh little Junior, you so lucky, big bad Maya is here to protect you. Someday we will meet when she is far, far away. You can count on it." Ray got off him and backed away keeping his eyes on Maya. He and his posse quickly got in the car and sped away. Andrew got up, gasping for air.

Maya ran toward him yelling, "I'm sorry. I'm so sorry"

"I'm okay, I'm okay. I gotta get home," he said.

But he wasn't okay. He was shaking like a leaf. Andrew could see the guys from the handball court coming toward him. It seemed like everybody in the park was staring at him. He jumped on his bike, but could barely pedal home. He could still feel Ray's knife pressed against his throat and hear Maya screaming that she was going to kill Ray. Andrew thought, I must have imagined this. Being jumped at knifepoint doesn't happen to guys like me. It was like a bad dream.

Maya kept texting him how sorry she was.

He just couldn't go home, so he stopped at Max's. His mother beamed. "Come in, come in. Max will be home any minute. He just went over to check out some new i Phone. Thank God he doesn't have enough money to buy another phone."

Andrew was still in shock, but he sat at the kitchen table with her. She insisted he have a bowl of homemade butternut squash soup and raisin bread. The hot soup tasted so good. It helped calm him. While he was eating the soup, Mrs. Donner leaned in toward him and said, "Well, Andrew, Max tells me you're not around any more because you have a girlfriend. Is that true?"

Andrew thought, Why did I ever come in here without Max? Now I'm trapped.

So he mumbled, "Well not really. She is kind of a new friend who needs a lot of help with Shakespeare."

"*Romeo and Juliet*, I hear."

Now Andrew was really regretting ever coming into Mrs. Donner's kitchen.

"Yes," he said and smiled.

"You know, Andrew it's none of my business, but since you

are like a son to me I want to say I think you are a little young yet for a girlfriend. But don't get me wrong. Girlfriends can be a wonderful thing. Already I worry about Max. What girl is going to put up with all this computer stuff?"

"You'd be surprised, Mrs. Donner. Lots of girls today love computers too."

Andrew was trying to move toward the side door as Max's mom continued, "Please bring that girlfriend of yours over to meet us. We're family. Some Friday, I'll make my double brownie mix. Does she like chocolate? Who doesn't?"

"Thanks, Mrs. Donner. I gotta go. Tell Max I stopped by."

When he got home he called Maya. She was crying and kept telling him it was her fault. He told her to meet him between their lunch periods. His lunch period was fifth, while she ate sixth period. They agreed to meet in the stairwell near the gym between fifth and sixth period.

When he hung up Andrew thought, What am I getting into? I know I'm playing with fire dating a girl with a brother like Cruz. But, Maya isn't just any girl. I want to protect her. I definitely want to see her again.

The next day Maya was waiting for him at the bottom of the stairs.

"Andrew, you're sure you're okay?"

Andrew nodded. "It isn't your fault that Ray is nuts."

Maya said, "I told that cockroach, Ray, if he hurts you in any way, I'll step on him big time. I know a lot about him that my brother doesn't."

"Listen, Maya, when I think about you holding that knife yesterday, what if Ray had grabbed it?"

"He'd be sorry, that's what. He'd have the scars to show for it. Trust me. I can take care of myself, especially against slime like Ray."

"It's not just about Ray. What if your brother finds out we were kissing in the park?

Your brother is pretty rough with you. I don't want you to get hurt."

"Listen, you can't let him keep us apart. Anyway, when my brother sees my English grade, he won't care about some kiss in the park. I am doing awesome in English now that you're helping me. On yesterday's quiz I got 100 because of you. I'll show him that. When you go to English class today, you'll get the next assignment sheet. We have to do a portfolio project on *Romeo and Juliet*. You wouldn't leave me before I finished my portfolio, would you, Brainiac?"

"We'll be more careful. Okay?" Andrew repeated.

"Okay."

During English just as Maya had said, Ski called out, "Portfolio Project." Some kids in Andrew's class bit their thumbs at Ski. Students had to choose five assignments from a list of creative suggestions. Some assignments involved a performance, like acting out a scene. You could work with one partner or in a group. Andrew chose the assignment that involved updating a key speech. Using Shakespeare's words he might create a rap or add another style music, like R&B. Both he and Max loved music. Maybe they could work on it together as a performance assignment. Since Max and he were in different classes, Andrew checked with Ski to see if they could work together.

"No problem," Ski said. "All my classes' portfolios will be part of a *Romeo and Juliet* exhibition in the school library. Actually, all the students will perform there so we can enjoy each other's creations. Come to Notes, that's the perfect place to work on your project."

Max already had the assignment sheet, so Andrew texted him: Want to team up on the portfolio project to create a song using Shakespeare's soliloquy? You control the sound and I'll work with the words. Ski is on board, says we can work on this at Notes.

Max's answer came within two minutes: Deal. We'll start tomorrow at Notes.

Surprisingly Maya became fixated on another assignment

called Catchy Quotes which required the students to record any quotes from the play that they found interesting, funny, or wise. Almost immediately Maya started texting Andrew her revisions of quotes from the play. They seemed to come day and night. She even texted him at 4:45 in the morning. The text read, "It is the East and Maya is the sun."

In his morning workout at the gym, Andrew stretched carefully. Today was Wednesday, when Cruz checked his progress.

"BB, let's see if you made as much progress as my sister did speaking Shakespeare. She showed me the 100 on the quiz. She said you helped her get that grade. Are you texting her the answers?"

"No, no," Andrew explained. "I told you already that Maya is smart."

"Smart mouth, that's what she's got. Don't say I didn't warn you. Now let me see you do the circuit."

At the bench press, Cruz asked, "Do you feel comfortable?"

As soon as Andrew nodded yes, Cruz added more weight. "Never let yourself get comfortable, BB."

At every station Cruz challenged Andrew to step up his program. Cruz just wasn't a guy you ignored. Andrew surprised himself with the amount of weight he could handle with Cruz watching him. Maybe it was the adrenalin. After the workout Andrew headed for school with a feeling of accomplishment.

Andrew was sitting in math class thinking about what Cruz had said about not getting comfortable when Maya texted him more quotes from *Romeo and Juliet.* Maya's text read, "Even if it's hot out, tomorrow wear gloves to the park. 'Oh that you were a glove upon my hand, that you might touch my cheek!' Are you thinking about my face or butt cheek, Andrew? I bet you're getting red now. You are so cute when you blush."

The next text came at midnight. "Goodnight, a thousand times goodnight."

In the morning, his mother said, "Is Max texting you in the middle of the night?"

"Yeah, mom. He's excited about some new iPhone."

"Really, Andrew, that's inappropriate. I wonder if his parents know he's up all hours of the night. That is unhealthy."

"Got it, mom. I'll tell him to lay off texting after 9:00. I don't know why my phone wasn't on vibrate. Sorry."

That day the topic in English class was fighting. Usually, the question of the day was on the board when the students entered the class. Today's question was: Are you a Montague, a Capulet, or your own person? More specifically, Ski wanted to know if a person had an obligation to watch a friend's back. If your friend got involved in a fight, did you have to fight too?

Most kids said they wanted to be individuals, but often friendships made them fight even if they didn't want to fight. Andrew was ashamed to admit that usually he was afraid to fight because he knew he'd lose.

When the period was over, a few kids stayed for he first meeting of Notes and more came in. There were about twenty kids in all, including Max.

Ski said, "We're going to take a field trip to the music room. Bring your laptop, I-pod, I pad, notebook or any receptacle for words and music." The music room was a huge room that housed a grand piano and many string and percussion instruments. As Andrew and Max got seated, Andrew heard beautiful music. Mr. Zucker, the music teacher, and a student were playing a duet on the piano.

"Chopin for sure," said Max.

Andrew was impressed. When it came to computers, music, or math, Max ruled.

Ski yelled, "Listen up. First, I want to welcome everyone to a brand new year at Notes. For the ninth graders who don't already know, this is the coolest club at John Glenn High School. Let me briefly tell you a little history of the club so you'll understand what makes it special.

"Notes began last year when a group of kids from the Creative Writing Club suggested using some of their poetry for song lyrics. You know how much I'm into poetry and music.

So, I approached Mr. Zucker, here," Ski said pointing to the grand piano where Mr. Zucker stood and took a bow. "He and I came up with a plan for a club where kids could write music or lyrics and put them together. We even have a group of kids experimenting with composing and using software on computers. Where are my techies?" A group of kids sitting next to window started cheering.

Max whispered to Andrew, "Those are my people."

"Not until we finish this song for the portfolio," Andrew replied.

Ski continued, "Every Wednesday we meet here for about an hour. During the first half, you're free to create--alone, with a partner, in groups--whatever. Mr. Zucker and I will walk around in case you need any help. The second part of the hour we will showcase. You read, sing, or perform and we, your audience, give you feedback. So, any questions?"

"What about snacks?"

"BYO –make them healthy. Be good to yourself. Okay, let's get started."

Andrew had been thinking about what speech to pick for their song. He leaned over toward Max and asked, "What do you think about a writing a song around a fight scene?"

"Yeah, a fight scene sounds like we could use drums and horns. I definitely don't want to do that balcony scene where you'd probably get involved with strings and flutes. One thing, you got to do most of the singing and talking. I don't like acting in public. Today in class we had to pair up with a girl and do part of the balcony scene. I just hated reading the lines in front of the class."

"No, problem," Andrew said, thinking Max had forgotten how he sang. Then Andrew asked, "What about when Romeo's friend, Mercutio, gets stabbed tying to defend Romeo? Mercutio's speech is really sly. It could make a cool song."

"Yeah, I can relate to that-- getting killed when your friend starts hanging out with a girl from a rough crowd who hates you."

Right then Andrew desperately wanted to tell Max about Ray holding the knife to his throat. Every time he closed his eyes to go to sleep Andrew felt the cold blade crawling up his neck toward his nose. Andrew just wasn't sure how Max would handle that. Maybe Max would tell his mom. Andrew was afraid to risk it.

"You wouldn't mind dying to defend me, would you?" Andrew asked. "We go way back. I'm sorry we haven't gotten to hang out as much as I'd like lately. I've been busy."

"Yeah. Maya Cruz in her skinny jeans can keep a boy busy."

"I'm helping her with English."

"Yeah, sure you are. I'm pitching in the World Series this month. Don't bother with the bullshit. When the fire dies down with your little tamale, maybe you'll be in the mood for pizza and computer games again.

"We'll get together to work on this project," Andrew promised. "I can only go so long without your mom's cooking."

Just being with Max made him feel better. He didn't want their friendship to end.

Ski opened up the mic so kids could practice. A kid named Foley started singing an R&B song he created using a refrain from the *Romeo and Juliet* quote. "Peace-I hate the word."

"Listen, Max, just like this guy used the line for a refrain, we could use Mercutio's line, 'a plague o' both your houses.' See if you can get a beat for that. We'll talk soon. I gotta go." Andrew had to leave to meet Maya in the park.

"Don't tell me. You're going to a party for *Cinco de Mayo*, even though it's only September."

"Yeah, something like that. See you."

As he walked up the park path, Maya rushed toward him, black eyes filled with anger, shiny hair loose and wild.

"Who is your Juliet? I will fight her right here."

"Maya, what are you talking about?"

"You went to English class today. You know we're up to the balcony scene."

"Yeah, so what?"

Maya said, "We're rewriting it in every day English. Then I'm suppose to act this out with some other guy. I don't want no other guy for Romeo. I have you. You are not getting another Juliet. I don't care if I have to get my program changed so I'm in your English class."

"Don't worry, I'm paired off with Sally Wareham. In fourth grade she drew a picture of me with a skinny stick body and a computer screen for a head. From the way she acted today, she hasn't changed her mind about me.

Maya sat on one of the park benches with the book on her lap. "Come sit next to me, I want you to say these lines to me, only me."

Maya had written in different colored inks all over the play. Andrew pointed and said, "You're not supposed to write in the book, Maya. It belongs to the school."

"Oh, Brainiac, you follow the rules way too much. I like this play. When I read words that are beautiful, I circle them in a beautiful color like aqua. The colors tell my feelings. Now say these lines to me, right now."

"Okay, okay." Andrew read aloud the line Maya was pointing to. "Did my heart love till now? I never saw true beauty till this night."

She was looking at the book, her lips parted slightly and her dark eyes shining.

"It's true Maya, you are beautiful. I like the way your black eyes flash your feelings. Today all the way from the bottom of the hill I could see how angry you were."

"Well, I'm still angry, especially about you sinning with another girl."

"Sinning? What play are you reading?" He shook his head.

"Turn the page." Maya read the lines out, "Then have my lips the sin that they have took." With that she kissed him right on the lips.

"I really like your kisses, but does the name Ray mean anything to you?"

"Oh Romeo, I could beat that skinny snot without my sword."

"If only Juliet were as tough as you," he said. But Andrew thought, If only I were as tough as you.

"By the way, texting me in the middle of the night isn't going over too well with my mother. She has supersonic hearing."

"What? Your mother doesn't like Shakespeare?"

"I'll send you a text in the middle of the night and see how your brother likes Shakespeare."

"My brother? Shakespeare understood him all right. You know in the play those guys, the Montagues and Capulets, they all love fighting. They don't even care what they are fighting about. Just like my brother, he smiles at any chance to fight--barefisted, brass knuckles, broken bottles, boxcutters, guns - whatever. I swear if he read this play, he'd have a razor-edged dagger."

"Why do you think he's like that?" Andrew asked.

"He's been fighting since he's a little kid in the streets of Mexico. When he came here from Juarez, he just continued, only harder, meaner."

"What about your parents?"

"My father and uncles came first. They worked as day laborers to get money for us to come. At first my father sent money. Then we didn't hear from him. My uncles said he disappeared at a street corner waiting for the boss to take him to some landscaping job. The police didn't do nothing. When my mother tried to sneak into the country to find him, she died. A year later my uncles sent money for my grandmother to come with my brother and me."

"Geeze, I'm sorry. How did your mother die?"

"She suffocated hiding in the back of a truck while she was trying to cross the border." Maya's voice shook and her black eyes glistened. Andrew put his arms around her and hugged her.

"My brother quit high school when he got here. He started hustling in the streets for nickels and dimes."

"That's why he wants you to do well in school. You know, get an education and a good job, as my mother constantly says."

Maya shook her head. "With my brother it's never about me. It's really about him. He wants me to get an education so I can run his business. He says a beautiful woman who is smart and well educated is a powerful weapon. I will be his. Not like your mother sitting in the bank making money."

"Don't think my mother doesn't work hard for a living. She went to college at night after my dad walked out. She worked harder than anyone to get her promotions. She's as tough as anyone." In a way, Maya and his mother were alike. It was a weird thought.

"She needs a lot of money to send your soccer- playing sister in her fine uniform to some big bucks university."

"Ally is a fighter too. She's playing in a game now. Come on. Let's watch her play."

"I don't fit in that world. We play soccer behind the bodega. We don't need uniforms."

"Come on, I'll race you there." He started to run down the park hill toward the athletic field when Maya jumped on his back, asking, "Do you think Romeo carried Juliet this way?"

"Juliet wasn't as fat as you."

Maya started kicking and screaming, "Romeo would never say such a thing,"Maya slid off his back and held Andrew's hand as they walked to the soccer field.

When they got to the bleachers, Maya became very quiet. Andrew felt the surprised stares of Max and some of the other kids. Maya whispered, "Your friend Max hates me. He stares at me like that in English class."

"He doesn't hate you. It's just that I use to spend a lot of my time with him. Now I spend it with you. You're much prettier."

Maya said, "I guess Romeo's good friend, Mercutio, would feel that way toward Juliet."

Andrew smiled. He found a seat for them off to the side. With the game tied 1-1 in the second half, Ally took a short pass from the midfielder and accelerated down the sideline. She had that quick first step and that was all she needed. Calm and focused, she followed the ball intently until she saw the goalie commit, and coolly rifled a shot into the far corner of the net. The crowd exploded, but the celebration didn't last long. On the next kick off the opposing forward was fouled in the box and was awarded a penalty kick. The forward drilled it and the score was again tied, 2-2.

With only two minutes to play Ally again found space and waved her right hand high into the air. A long pass landed at her feet and she deftly shed the fullback, but a second defender was closing in. Ally lofted a high cross to her center, who headed it in for the game winner as the clock was winding down. Andrew jumped to his feet and cheered. Maya screamed, "Yeah, Ally!"

Going home, Maya conceded, "Your sister is awesome in soccer."

That night while Andrew watched TV in the den, he could hear his mother talking to Ally while they cleaned up the kitchen.

"There's a rumor at work that the next district manager is going to be a twenty- nine year- old woman who is with the bank only a few years. She's very sharp, with no husband or kids to hold her back. She could easily be the company's first female CEO."

"What are you saying, Mom, I shouldn't have kids 'cause they'll hold me back? I want to have kids."

"Naturally, with children to manage, your life becomes more complicated. But, you are excellent at compartmentalizing. Look at how well you handle your schoolwork and sports. There is no reason you can't have children and a high -powered career too. You know, some single women even use sperm donors to have kids."

Ally was quiet. Then she said, "Mom, do you remember Bryan, that geeky little kid from down the block? He grew up to become one gorgeous guy. He's really easy to talk to and be with. Maybe I'd like to marry a guy like him and raise a family together."

"I know who you mean," her mother snapped. "Don't be

ridiculous. He's just a chick magnet. You don't want him ruining your life. He doesn't even strike me as very smart."

Andrew turned off the TV, wondering just where he fit in his mother's scheme of men. If men were just chick magnets and women didn't even need men to reproduce, maybe his mother thought men would soon be extinct. She probably was relieved.

He wondered: just how would his mother handle Cruz? How would he react to her?

Just the thought of it made him laugh. He had to stop imagining that. Tomorrow was Wednesday and his third meeting to work out with Cruz. Andrew needed to be well rested for that, so he went to bed.

CHAPTER 4

"Is that a bicep I'm starting to see?" Cruz observed the next morning, "You can add some weight now."

Cruz grabbed two 25- pound plates and put one on each side of the 45-pound bar. That was 95 lbs in all. Andrew broke out into a cold sweat. He didn't know if he could handle this. With Cruz spotting him, adrenaline and fear kicked in as he strained to do eight repetitions.

"Now that you have some muscle, I have a job for you. You know, earn some Benjamins. Buy my sister a little glitter. Maybe you can get her a diamond stud bookmark?"

"What kind of job?" Andrew could barely speak, let alone think.

I need a nerdy guy like you to carry some cash for my sale on Friday night at the park. You do know about my sale every Friday night, parkside?"

Andrew nodded. He could feel the red climbing up his neck.

"No need to get nervous, BB," Cruz said, putting his hand on Andrew's shoulder. "All you have to do this time is stand against the fence. Steely will handle the goods and stash the cash in your knapsack. I bet you never had any significant paper in there. But you'll have to take out all those books. Meet Steely at the gas station at 6:00 Friday night."

"Okay," Andrew said quickly.

As soon as Andrew got out on the street, he hurried. He didn't want to be late to school. As he entered the building, he texted Maya to meet him in the stairwell before lunch. Andrew felt tense. He was proud that Cruz considered him tough enough to team with him. But Andrew knew this could be dangerous. He needed to talk to Maya. He felt better just seeing her coming down the stairs as he waited for her.

As soon as she got close to him, she asked, "Are you all right? What happened?"

"Your brother wants me to hold the cash while Steely sells on Friday night at the park."

Immediately she whispered, "No way! Are you loco? Carry cash for my brother? Why do you think the police check the kids' pockets? They identify the pushers by the amount of money they carry."

"Maya, you of all people know I can't say no to your brother. You know what he'll do to me?"

"I know what he'll do to you if you say yes. The only advice I can give to you is, run, baby, run and take me with you."

"You're talking crazy. We're fourteen years old. Where are we going to run?"

"We'll figure it out. You really want to know why I want you to run? Because I love you."

"Love me?" Andrew said. He didn't know what to say. He felt so much for Maya. He had never said those words to any girl. They were so special. He just wasn't prepared to say them here.

"Yeah, Andrew. Love you and I'm the one who's not supposed to understand the play." He quickly kissed her. Kids were passing them to go up the stairs.

"Maya, I wanted it to be a special place like under the stars, not in the school stairwell. I need words like Romeo said to Juliet when I tell you I love you. But, I do love you."

"You do! I knew it," said Maya throwing her arms around him.

"Wait a minute," he said, pulling her arms from around his

neck. "It just seems so complicated. I just gotta figure out what to do now."

"We will figure it out. I'll call you later. Don't worry," said Maya, pushing her way up the stairs.

As hard as Andrew tried, he couldn't figure a way out. What were his options? Tell his mom or tell Cruz. Andrew wished he could talk to Ski, but didn't know how to approach him. Maybe today after the weekly meeting of Notes he could have a chance to talk with Ski. After last period Andrew waited for Max to walk to the music room. Inside the music room, kids were slowly taking seats. Some were talking, others listening to their iPods, while some were already writing.

Max opened his binder and took out the *Romeo and Juliet* Portfolio assignment sheet. said, "So, what do we got so far? Last week you said I could use Mercutio's line, 'A plague o' both your houses.' But I don't really get it."

"Did you read Mercutio's speech at the beginning of Act III where he's got Romeo's back and Tybalt stabs him?"

"Sort of," Max replied.

"Well, Tybalt stabs Mercutio. At first, Mercutio's trying to look cool, pretending not to be hurt. But, he gives the audience a big clue to the truth when he says, 'Ask for me tomorrow, and you shall find me a grave man.' Grave-- get it, Max? Buried?"

"I get it Andrew," said Max reading the speech intently. "Sounds like this dude Mercutio is really angry."

"Yeah, he blames the families. That's why he says, 'A plague o' both your houses'."

"Yep, there's a lot of anger here. That's what I have to know to create the sound, an angry tone for certain. All right, I'm out of here."

"Aren't you going to stay to see the performances?"

"We got our own performance to worry about. I want to check out what's happening in the computer room on the way out."

"Call me when you got the beat set," said Andrew.

Actually Andrew was glad to be by himself. He enjoyed

listening to the kids experimenting with words and music. A few kids played guitars while their partners experimented with different lyrics. When Andrew listened to the chords they reminded him of waves in the ocean. He thought of the words like a seagull riding the waves up and down. He found the music and the words exciting and comforting. He even smiled, imagining Shakespeare wearing a T shirt and jeans, bringing his words to play on a rock or an R&B sound.

After the meeting was over, Andrew waited in the room for all the kids to leave. Ski looked at him and smiled like they met to talk everyday.

"What's up, Andrew?"

"You have a minute to talk?"

"Sure."

Andrew was too embarrassed to talk about himself, so he blurted out, "Do you think Romeo and Juliet ever had a chance of getting out of that mess?"

"What could they have done?" asked Ski.

"Maybe Romeo could have refused to fight Tybalt. Mercutio didn't have to be the wing man. Maybe they could have tried talking to their parents, or planned an escape."

"Maybe," said Ski. "Life has got a lot of possibilities." Then Ski paused a minute and asked, "Is this conversation really just about Romeo and Juliet?"

"Nah, you know Maya Cruz. She's in your first period class?"

"Well, I know her as my student. Not quite the way you know her, from what I hear from the kids at school."

"Yeah, everybody's watching. Even my best friend, Max Donner, is pissed off about it."

"The important thing is not what everybody knows or thinks. It's what you think. So what do you think about Maya?"

"I never knew a girl like her. I never knew anyone quite like her. She's funny and crazy and I really like being with her. It's her brother I'm not so sure of."

Ski said, "He's got quite a dangerous reputation."

"Yeah, and a lot of it's true. He's helping me work out at the gym. But, I don't know; he keeps warning me not to get to close to Maya."

Andrew wanted to level with Ski about the drug sales and how he wished he could find a way out of it, but somehow he couldn't.

"What does your family think about all this? Let me guess, they don't know?"

Andrew nodded, "How did you guess?"

"Not even your sister, Ally?"

"She knows a little."

"I'm sure. She is smart. I had her in ninth grade when she was the only freshman on varsity soccer."

"That's her. She is smart, but I got to figure this out myself."

"Seems to me you got a pretty good head on your shoulders, and you're looking stronger these days."

"Thanks, like I said, I've been working out."

"If you want to talk again, I'm usually here after class."

"Yeah, maybe I will. Thanks."

Initially, talking to Ski made Andrew feel a lot better. But by Friday, Andrew still didn't know how to get out of helping Cruz. So at 6 p.m. on Friday he dressed in black jeans, tee, and hoodie. He told his mom he was eating at Max's again. Andrew's knees started to shake when he saw the Mustang parked at the gas station.

Only Steely was in the car. "BB, this is real simple." He took a wad of cash and stuffed it in Andrew's backpack. "Stay cool. I'll open the store. This is penny candy, just to give the customer a taste, bring in the business. Get it?"

Andrew nodded.

Steely continued, "I tell you what the customer owes. They will give you the cash. You keep the money until I signal. If something goes wrong, you don't know whose backpack it is. Someone you never saw gave it to you and said they'd be right back."

When they arrived, at the park, Steely pulled into the lot

behind the picnic area. It was hopping. Kids hanging out and cars pulling in and out, music blaring. As soon as they turned in, Andrew saw the pulsating red light of the cop car.

"Bail," Steely yelled.

Andrew opened the car door, grabbed his knapsack, and threw it under a silver SUV parked diagonally across from them. License # JNL6062, he noted. As Andrew started running toward the back gate of the lot, a black Honda flashed its lights at him.

His mother's car - but when he opened the door, his sister Ally was behind the wheel. She was already making a U turn to leave as he jumped into the seat.

"Shit, Alley. Thank God you're here." His body was in a cold sweat and his fingers shook as he texted Maya telling her where he hid the cash.

"Oh my God, Andrew. Who are you texting? What is going on here? I told you stay out of the park," Ally yelled.

"Ally, why are you here?"

"After your last Friday night escapade, I was worried, so I followed you. Good thing I did. What's going on here, Andrew?"

He knew he had to come clean to his sister, at least partly. He said, "Um, well, a couple of weeks ago when I was working out in the gym, that motorcycle guy Cruz offered to help me with my workout."

"That hood wants to help you for nothing?" Ally asked

"As a payback I'm helping his sister, Maya, with Shakespeare assignments. She's really nice. We've become friends."

"I didn't see her in that Mustang, Andrew."

"No, I was supposed to meet her at the gas station. We were going to hang out together at the park. But she couldn't make it. So her brother's friend just dropped me off here."

"Well you look pretty stressed for a guy who is just hanging out. I hear you using the word friend to describe these kids. Are these the kids you want for friends?"

He kept looking back, asking, "Ally, are the cops behind us?"

Ally replied, "Why should they be? Since when is working out and tutoring against the law?"

Andrew shrugged. "Where are we going?" he asked.

"Lickety Splits. You didn't have dinner, did you? I'll tell Mom I saw you and Max there and brought you home."

"Thanks, Ally."

"Listen," she said. "When the cops call, they won't be calling me. Promise me you'll do the right thing. Andrew, promise you won't see these kids any more."

"Okay, Okay, I promise."

"This is serious. You have to tell Mom about this or I will."

While he ate his burger at the ice cream shop, his phone beeped, but he couldn't answer it until he was home and alone in his bedroom.

The text from Maya said Steely found the money and her brother would meet him tomorrow at 7 AM in the gym.

Tomorrow, shit! Tomorrow was Saturday. He usually slept late. Tomorrow at the gym he'd have to tell Cruz he wanted out. What was the big deal? He wasn't even really in. Ally had said in the car that he should do the right thing. Aside from throwing some money under a car, he really hadn't done anything.

The next morning Cruz was sitting on his Harley, outside the gym, all smiles. "Well here's the man. You not only got rid of the evidence, you returned it to its rightful owner. Cool under fire. For your fine service, here's a little paper." Cruz slipped five $100 bills into Andrew's hand.

"No, no, that's all right," Andrew said quickly.

"The money. This is what it's all about. Remember that." Then he put his arm around Andrew. "You're all right, BB. See you Wednesday."

Cruz roared off on the bike, hammering nails on noise into the morning light. Andrew felt a rush, an excitement. Cruz had been proud of him. He looked at the $500 in his hand. He never had seen that much money, no less had it in his hand. One of Cruz' sayings was, "Cash is king."

Andrew taped the money under his desk in his room. It was impossible to hide anything from his mom, who even cleaned the light bulbs. He stuck around home that weekend, doing chores and homework, aware of Ally watching him.

On Monday he took 100 dollars from under the desk to buy Maya a gift. First he thought about buying her a telescope, but that would involve getting someone to drive him to the store. Andrew thought, What might be beautiful, like the stars? Flowers, he decided. He texted Maya to meet him at the park a little later that usual, and on the way he stopped at the florist and bought twelve long-stem red roses. On the little white card Andrew wrote, "That which we call a rose by any other name would smell as sweet."

Maya's black eyes widened when she first saw them.

"For me, Andrew? How beautiful. I love them."

"Well, I got the money from your brother for Friday night. I didn't even do much."

"Wait," she yelled. "You bought these for me with dope money? I told you I didn't want you working for him." She started snapping the heads off each rose.

"Stop, Maya, what are you doing?"

She threw them on the ground. The beautiful red roses with broken necks lay in the dirt. She yelled, "Save your money for flowers for your funeral if you work for my brother." Crying hysterically she ran through the park, while Andrew kicked the remains of roses on the ground. All that money wasted, he thought. It wasn't like he ever had much money. He shouldn't have bothered buying her anything.

What was even more ridiculous, he had planned on giving the rest of the money to help Ally. Senior year was expensive, but now he felt too ashamed to even consider it. Maya had told him not to get involved with her brother, and Andrew had promised Ally he would stop seeing Cruz.

Why couldn't he quit?

Wednesday rolled around real quick. Andrew went to the gym early, hoping Cruz wouldn't show. But he was already there in the middle of his workout. He was all business and watched intently as Andrew did each exercise. At the end he said, "Good job, BB. Meet Steely Friday, same time, same place. Let's just hope the cops don't spoil the party."

Leaving the gym, at first, Andrew was excited by Cruz's praise. For the first time he felt confident. But Andrew worried, too. He was getting in too deep. What if he couldn't get out? It was a scary feeling.

The following Friday night, he got ready to hook up with Steely again. Right from the start the job went smoothly. Since Ally's big game, the showcase, was one week away, she was practicing every night. His mother went straight to the field from work, so he didn't have to invent any visits with Max. As he walked home from school, he got a text that told him the deal was going down under the train trestle. Andrew felt weird getting a text about drug deals while his classmates were texting about their weekend plans, like watching football. But at six, he met Steely at the gas station. They drove together to the train trestle.

Andrew got out of the car with his hood up. As Steely dealt the drugs, he called out a price. All kinds of kids handed the cash to Andrew. He had seen most of these kids in the hall at school.

Some seemed scared of him as they handed him the money. Andrew enjoyed the power. Some of the kids wearing T- shirts and jackets from the local college were dropping Benjamins left and right. He was counting the money in his head and figured it was over six grand by the time Steely gave him the signal to close up.

On the way home Steely said, "Fine work tonight. Listen, I gotta swing by Cruz's. He's got a problem downtown." They drove about three miles south of the Ave. when the car slowed down in front of a big beige stucco Spanish Mission style home. Steely leaned on the horn. Andrew strained to see if he could get a glimpse of Maya. Nothing slipped by Cruz, who was waiting out front.

"Sorry, BB, I got her locked up in the tower. When the stars come out, she will be on the balcony. Try climbing up and see what happens." Cruz laughed loudly as he jumped into the car. Steely drove to the bus depot where homeless people, many of them strung out, were milling around outside. It was chilly for early October, and they looked cold.

"That's him!" Cruz yelled. In a few seconds Cruz and Steely jumped out of the car with the engine still running. They shoved a skinny, shaking guy wearing filthy clothes to the ground. Andrew heard his skull hit the cement. Steely stepped on his neck while Cruz emptied out his pockets. Then they both started kicking him in the head. The man screamed out in pain and lay in the street crying uncontrollably. Andrew had never heard a grown man cry like that.

Quickly they jumped back in the car. Both of them laughing like this was some kind of joke. Andrew felt sick to his stomach. What if he vomited in the Mustang?

"How about some steaks and lobster, BB? Steely said you more than held your own tonight." How could they be laughing and talking about eating? Andrew wondered. What was the matter with them? He tried to stay calm.

"Nah, I gotta go," Andrew said. "I can catch the bus home from here."

Cruz took a brown envelope and stuffed it into Andrew's shirt. "See Steely next Friday, same time and place." When Andrew got to the corner, he took ten Benjamins out of the envelope. There was no way he could hide this much money. On the way home on the bus, Andrew worried about what to do with so much cash.

The bus left him off at the Ave. not far from his house. Walking home, Andrew saw a lot of people smoking in front of a local church. Members from an AA meeting. Kind of sad, they were smoking, trying to stop drinking. Andrew slipped by the crowd and tried the church door. It was open. He went into the church vestibule and crammed the $1,000 into the poor box.

CHAPTER 5

The next morning Andrew awoke thinking about how cruel Cruz had been to that homeless guy. But he couldn't help wondering what eating dinner at some posh restaurant downtown with Cruz and Steely would have been like. He could envision trays of appetizers: calamari, jumbo shrimp and stuffed clams and an entrée with gigantic red lobsters, thick juicy steaks, and chocolate mousse with turrets of whipped cream. He almost could hear Cruz and Steely laughing.

"Andrew, get up," his mother called. "I need to talk to you. Now."

His mother's perfect posture as she stood by the kitchen sink put Andrew on the defensive.

"What's up, Mom?"

"Embarrassment – that's what's up."

"What are you talking about?"

"I'm talking about Mrs. Donner and my conversation in the supermarket this morning. She said her family missed your visits on Friday nights, but she understood since you have a girlfriend. Then she asked me how I liked Maya Cruz. Can you imagine I had never even heard of Maya Cruz? When I was speechless, she said I probably was concerned, especially with Maya's brother's reputation with drugs. Andrew, who are these people? How could you have chosen this kind of girl to date? You are much too young for any girlfriend, no less a girl like this."

"Relax, Mom. I just met her."

"How did you meet her and that criminal brother?"

"Well, you know when I started to work out in the gym? Her brother offered to help me with my workout if I helped his sister with her assignments in English class. She was having trouble understanding Shakespeare, and she's in Sikorski's first period English class."

"That's it."

"Yeah."

"Don't lie to me. You have been lying to me for weeks now."

"I had to lie to you."

"Why is that?"

"I knew you never would let me hang out with Maya. She is really interesting."

"Interesting? Oh, please," said his mother while raising her eyebrows. Andrew added loudly, "There are other kids in school besides nerds who ass kiss the teacher for 90's to get that Ivy League education and become CEO's of corporate America."

"Well, Andrew, for some reason you want to be a bottom dweller."

"Maya is smart in a lot of ways."

"I bet she is, but she is not teaching my son any more. You are forbidden to see her or her brother again. Do you understand?"

"Mom, do you understand? That I hate school and this house" Andrew screamed, slamming his fist into his palm.

"Well, that is most unfortunate for you, because from now on home and school are the only places you will be. I will drive you to school in the morning and you will come directly home after school. I trusted you and you broke that trust. I should have known better."

"Yeah, Mom, never trust a man."

"Watch what you say to me, Andrew. I'm warning you. From now on you are on a very short leash. You will use the computer only for school related assignments. Make sure you move the TV that's in your bedroom into the den tonight. Hand over your phone now."

Andrew took his phone from out of his jeans pocket and hurled it at the wall. "I hate you!" he screamed.

"Pick up that phone now and hand it to me along with your iPod before I throw both of them into the garbage. If you are wondering what you will be doing with your spare time, you will begin by cleaning. Start with the toilets in the bathrooms. Now!"

"Mom, men doing housework, this is your dream come true. Make sure you get a photo."

She stared at him as cold as ice. "If you ever thought of considering yourself a fine specimen of a man, believe me, you are not one today. It's Saturday, remember? I work today and so will you from now on. The bleach is under the sink. The list of chores for today is on the fridge."

Actually doing the chores was the easy part of the punishment. When Andrew completed them, he felt lost. Then he decided to use the time to do homework. He definitely had to work on the song lyrics for the *Romeo and Juliet* portfolio. Max must be pretty pissed by now.

Andrew read Mercutio's speech and thought about telling this part of the story in the song. The first verse, Andrew decided, needed to introduce Mercutio, Romeo's friend who was watching Romeo's back out in the square in ancient Verona. What thanks did Mercutio get? He got stabbed by Tybalt, Romeo's hated enemy.

In the second verse Andrew focused on showing how Mercutio tried to hide his wound, but quickly realized he was dying. In the last verse Andrew dramatized Mercutio blaming both sides of the fight for his death.

Andrew wondered, In every fight, are both parties to blame? Mercutio believed that.

What had Max said about capturing a sound to match Mercutio's mood? What words would describe angry? Andrew decided to emphasize the word "scratch." Andrew liked saying that word out loud. He included Shakespeare's descriptive words, "worms' meat" to dramatize Mercutio's death. Death provided the horror in the song.

Alone in the quiet of his room without his phone, Andrew thought he would go crazy. If they only had a land line, he could call Maya from the house. He missed Maya so much. When he closed his eyes, he could see her hanging upside down on the swings. He longed to touch her hair and hear her laugh. Maybe she was right--they should run away. What did Cruz say would happen if he climbed into her bedroom window?

The day dragged on endlessly. Ally went out with friends. He and his mother hardly spoke during dinner. Having run out of ideas to keep busy, Andrew went to sleep early.

At midnight, even though his mother had his phone, he thought he heard a beep. So he whispered, "Good night. A thousand times good night."

On Sunday morning he woke up feeling like he was going to jump out of his skin. He needed to exercise. If he couldn't continue working out with Cruz at the gym, he had to try to follow the routine at home. He wasn't going to lose the muscle he had gained.

Andrew remembered that his father had left a set of weights behind. He thought he saw them recently in a box in the garage or was it the basement? After going past shovels and rakes and into boxes of Christmas decorations, he still couldn't find them.

He considered calling his dad to find out where the weights were stored. But he would have to ask his mom to use her phone, and he felt awkward calling his dad now. They hadn't really talked at any length since Andrew's birthday in July. After his father first remarried and moved upstate, he would call Andrew every week. But the conversations about school and sports were so forced, they seemed so pointless. They always ended with his dad making some kind of excuses for not visiting. Though it wasn't all his dad's fault. Sometimes his dad left messages that Andrew didn't bother to answer. Gradually, he stopped calling except for special occasions.

No, it would definitely be too weird calling his father now. He would have to explain why he was grounded. It was easier to keep looking. So Andrew continued his search and finally found the weights buried under paints and an old ladder. He cleared a space by the washing machine and set up the weights and an exercise mat. Using Cruz's plan, he adapted a new workout routine for himself.

Monday morning he was desperate to go to school. He wondered how Cruz would react when he heard why Andrew hadn't shown on Friday night. Imagine Cruz hearing Andrew was grounded – how lame. During breakfast and the drive to school, he and his mother didn't exchange a single word. Silence: a weapon his mother used so well. Today he didn't care if he ever talked to his mother again.

Inside the school building, Andrew went directly to Maya's first period. Max was already in his seat and gave Andrew the high sign.

"Hey, Max, which seat is Maya's?"

"First row, last seat. She's got a great view of what's happening in the hall. We got to get together to work on the song. After school at my house, whenever. My mom will be so happy."

"Sure thing, I worked on the lyrics a little over the weekend. I don't have my phone. It's a real drag. That's why I'm leaving Maya a note. Talk to you later."

Andrew didn't have the time or the energy to tell Max about the fallout from their mothers' meeting in the supermarket. Going right to Maya's desk, inside he left a handwritten note saying: Busted by mom – grounded – no phone.

After second period, Maya was waiting outside Andrew's math class. He quickly filled Maya in on what happened with his mother. Then he reminded her, "Make sure you tell your brother so he knows I didn't skip Friday on purpose."

"I'm glad you skipped Friday. Do you think that my brother

cares you're grounded? He doesn't believe in grounding. He says that's for white people. That's why if I don't do what he wants, he just beats the shit out of me. Listen, Andrew, what's important here is that you understand that we are going to have to fight your mother and my brother and who knows who else for us to stay together. Are you willing to fight?"

"I guess so," he said, amazed at Maya's toughness. I have to be tough too, he thought, to stay with Maya

"You guess so?"

"Okay, Okay, I'll fight. I miss you so much, Maya."

"Cut history today. I'll meet you in the stairwell near the cafeteria. I know a place where we can hide."

"Cut class?"

"When are we going to see each other if we don't cut?"

"My mom is so angry now. I can't image what she'll do when she finds out I cut."

"I'll see you seventh period in the stairwell near the cafeteria."

History was seventh period. As soon as Andrew walked past the room he felt everybody knew he was going to cut. At the bottom of the stairwell, Maya was waiting.

She waited till the hall was clear and then led him into an empty storeroom. They ate chips and drank soda that she had brought from the cafeteria.

"Isn't this fun?" asked Maya giving Andrew some chips

Not really, Andrew thought. He was too nervous expecting the deans to find them any minute. "Listen, Maya, you never told me what your brother said about me not helping Steely on Friday."

"I don't care what he thinks. I'm glad you couldn't go. I don't want you involved with my brother. He will destroy the honest, good person you are."

"You like that about me?" asked Andrew.

"I love that about you."

Andrew hugged her and said, "To tell you the truth, Maya,

I was glad I couldn't go. I just don't want your brother to be angry."

Maya said, "My brother is always pissed off at something or someone. But I texted him at lunch time that you were grounded. He said that you weren't as smart as you thought you were or you would have cut your mother's apron strings by now. He expects you to work with Steely on Friday. He's adding more weight to your program on Wednesday and you better be ready. He says when you work for him there is no time off for bad behavior."

Andrew had to laugh. Cruz was crazy.

When the bell rang, Maya asked, "Was that so scary? I'll wait for you after second period, *manana.* My third period teacher doesn't care if I'm late."

Then Maya came toward him, extending both arms. They kissed. Andrew said, "Right now I feel like you and I could be together forever. Then I remember we're cutting, and I think about my mother and your brother."

Maya said, "Stop. You think too much. You've got to learn to live dangerously. It can be fun."

"*Manana*, loco girl," Andrew replied.

As soon as he left Maya, he felt depressed. He wished he could just go home and play computer games with Max and have some of Mrs. Donner's chocolate brownies. By ninth period, when it was time to write in his daily journal entry for English class, Andrew only had the strength to write in huge letters GROUNDED FOR LIFE! Walking up and down the aisles, Ski spotted the entry and simply put his hand on Andrew's shoulder.

But at the end of the class Ski said to Andrew, "I want to get my laptop from my car. I'll walk out with you." Then Ski looked Andrew in the eyes and smiled, saying, "Okay, I was just curious what behavior merited grounding for life."

"Well, you already know about Maya and her brother. Saturday my mom found out that I knew them and went ballistic. I didn't even tell her the details."

"Cruz does have a dangerous reputation. Is there any chance of you ending that?"

Andrew hesitated, "I kind of work for him."

"Kind of?"

"All right, I worked for him a couple of times. After last night with my mother, I don't know if I want to quit. At least Cruz treats me like an adult. If I stopped working for Cruz, I would have to stop seeing Maya. I'm not giving up Maya."

"Have you told your mother this?"

"I can't."

"Why not?"

"She would have to listen."

Ski paused and then said, "I'm a real good listener. How about we meet Friday during my prep period. What do you have then?"

"Gym."

"All those muscles you now have will earn you a pass from gym class on Friday. I'll set it up with your gym teacher."

"Okay, talk to you then," Andrew said as he left the building. Just knowing that he would talk to Ski on Friday helped Andrew face going home. When he got inside his house, Ally wasn't there. She was practicing every day now, since her showcase game was Friday night.

Andrew missed her. Even though Ally worked hard she kept things light and happy. The house seemed so much better when she was home. Today with his mother's list of chores, Andrew was almost too busy to worry. His mother made it very clear that all homework was to be finished first. Then he started vacuuming and getting the dinner ready, peeling the vegetables before his mother got home from work. At dinner, thankfully, Ally dominated the conversation.

"After practice the coach told me I am right on game. That I shouldn't have any problems in the game on Friday."

His mother looked at her and said, "Ally, you've worked hard since you started soccer in second grade. Just be yourself.

That is more that enough. Finish your homework and get to bed early. Rest is important. Andrew will clear the table and load the dishwasher."

Ally said, "I'll do it. It's my turn."

His mother insisted, saying, "Andrew will do it and he'll do it alone." Ally left, giving Andrew kind of a half smile. But when Andrew carried the dirty dishes into the kitchen, he noticed the counter had been already cleared and cleaned and the stove wiped down. On the window of the stove Ally had drawn a little heart with a message, "I luv my bro," written inside. Andrew smiled. He could always count on Ally.

All week long, he kept waiting for the detention notice for cutting history. When it never came, Maya took this as a signal for a cutting free-for-all. But Andrew refused to cut, seeing her only for a few minutes between classes. On sunny days Maya cut classes to hit the handball courts.

On his way home he passed by the park, hoping to catch a glimpse of her. She was on the court serving low and fast. Hector, one of the regulars, was losing badly, and the other guys were on his case. When he was able to return the ball, Maya had him running right to left and then back. She could hit with either hand and moved like a cat.

Watching her play, Andrew wondered if he could keep up with her demands. He didn't like cutting class. To have time with Maya this week, he had also already missed the meeting of Notes. But, his mother had taken all his free time. When were they supposed to see each other? It wasn't just his relationship with Maya that was suffering. He couldn't even go to the gym this week to work out with Cruz. Don't be such a loser, he told himself. When he got home he forced himself to work out hard with his father's weights.

On Friday, Maya was waiting outside the school for him in the rain. Maya said, "I have a surprise for you. Today I am going to take you to my secret places."

"How are you going to do that? Remember I'm grounded and have to go right home?"

"You have to get over your ridiculous fear of cutting."

"I can't today. Tonight is Ally's showcase game."

"For a brainiac, sometimes you act very dumb. Today your mother will be so busy with Ally, she won't have time to think about what you're doing."

"I'm supposed to meet Ski today."

"Andrew you have to decide. Do you want to be with me or not? Today is all we have. Listen, I have it all set up. Go and have your attendance taken. Then meet me at the side door. Don't worry, I'll have you home in time to hook up with Steely."

"How am I going to meet Steely with my mother on my case? I'm never going to be able to sneak out now."

"Listen, Andrew, I told you not to work for my brother. Now that you're in, all I can say is, you better show up tonight."

Thinking about trying to sneak past his mother to meet Steely made him feel sick. And he just couldn't miss Ally's game. He had to be there for her. With one butt he couldn't be in two places. He felt like he was testing the theory about being in two places at the same time when he swiped his ID to have his attendance taken for the day and within seconds walked out the side door of the school.

Andrew couldn't believe how many kids were doing the same thing. There was Maya, wearing her short coat and waving wildly. "Hurry, so we catch the next train. I'm taking you home for lunch."

"Home, where your brother lives, and where your grandmother might just realize you cut since you're home at 9:30 a.m.?"

"Relax, my brother is never home on Friday. He does business on Fridays. Today my grandmother went shopping with her friend in the city."

"Phone her just to make sure."

Maya rolled her eyes at him while she called. Even though

Maya was speaking Spanish with her grandmother, Andrew could tell things were going as planned by the tone in Maya's voice.

"She won't be home till dinner. No *problema*."

They could hear the train coming. Andrew was surprised how fast Maya could run.

"You should try out for track," he said, catching his breath.

"I get a lot of practice running away from my brother. You don't want him to catch you if he's angry, believe me."

"I do," Andrew said, holding her hand as they stepped inside the train.

The train rocked Maya and Andrew as they sat side by side. She put her head on his shoulder. Seated next to the window, Andrew could see the neighborhood changing, even though Maya only lived two stops away from him. There the streets were more crowded. More factories and buildings lined the streets.

Maya suddenly sat up. "Andrew, I want to talk about the discussion in English class yesterday."

"What about it?"

"Yesterday we acted out the scene where Juliet tells her father she won't marry Paris, the guy her father has picked out for her. Her father gets rough with her and says--here, I wrote it down." Maya took out her phone and accessed her quote journal. Juliet's father screams, 'Hang, beg, starve, die in the streets. For, by my soul, I'll never acknowledge thee'."

"That's pretty rough," Andrew agreed.

"The kids in my class said no parent would act like that today. They don't know my brother. If I crossed him he would throw me out and wouldn't care if I starved or died on the streets. Sometimes I wish I had that fake poison that Juliet had that fools people into thinking you are dead. Then I could run away."

"I've been thinking about what you said about your brother controlling your future. Life is different for us than it was for Romeo and Juliet. They could only run away on those slow-ass donkeys that couldn't take them very far. Today we travel by airplanes. In a few hours you could be anywhere in the world where no one ever heard of your brother. You could be starting a whole new life. There's a lot of hope in airplanes. You don't need any fake poison to get away."

When Andrew put his arm around her, Maya started climbing onto Andrew's lap. What are you doing now, loco girl?"

"I'm looking for airplanes out this window. You're right. I never thought of hope in airplanes."

"You could have just asked me to change seats."

"You don't want me sitting on your lap? Oh, Brainiac, you let your chances go by. Too late. Our stop is next."

When the doors opened, they stepped onto a station where the walls were covered in graffiti. The elevated train covered the main street giving it a dark, spooky feel. The streets in her neighborhood were narrow, littered with paper cups and plastic wrappers. The sidewalks were crowded with shoppers, day workers, mothers with kids.

The day was damp and gray. Maya said, "I'm cold. Let's get a coffee at the bodega where I go every morning. Ernesto is my other boyfriend. He knows exactly how to fix my coffee. Don't be jealous."

Andrew enjoyed the feel of the neighborhood. He said, "I like the noise, the people." Maya smiled, "It's life on the move, Brainiac."

As soon as they got inside the crowded bodega, Ernesto who was old enough to be her grandfather saw Maya and yelled, *"Buenos dias, Bella,* one small coffee, light and sweet, right? What about your friend?" Andrew ordered a cherry Gatorade.

While they sat on stools at the counter, Maya said, "I have a little tour planned of some my favorite places that I don't take anybody else. The first place I want to show you is right up the block."

Holding hands, they walked up the block until Maya stopped at an old red brick school. "There is PS 6, where I went to elementary school. I hated it except for one thing. Come, I'll show you."

In the back of the school was a large field, mostly overgrown with weeds.

Maya said, "The school ran out of money so they don't have the program no more. When I was in the fourth grade, every kid was given a patch of dirt to grow flowers. I grew pink flowers, zinnias. First we planted seeds in a hothouse. Then I knelt on the cold, hard ground and dug a space in the dirt for my plants. I still remember how I loved digging in the dirt." Andrew smiled.

"Come on, Andrew, dig with me in the dirt." They knelt on the ground. From her knapsack, Maya took out two little spoons and gave one to Andrew. Maya turned over the hard cold soil. "I carried these just to show you." Deeper down the dirt became soft, rich, black soil. "Oh, Andrew. Isn't it beautiful? You can even smell the earth."

"I don't know," Andrew said, feeling silly digging in a field of weeds in the cold, rainy autumn day. He said, "When I was very little I do remember helping my dad rake leaves in the backyard. He would pile up huge mounds and throw me in the leaves."

"I'm always talking about my brother. You never talk about your dad. Did he just up and leave?"

"I'm not so sure. I was just four when he and my mom split. I remember them fighting a lot. It's strange that I think about them yelling, because actually my dad is an easygoing guy, too easygoing. My mom just walked all over him."

"What do you mean?"

"He used to come visit us every week. My mom didn't want him around us. All my mom cares about is that his child support check comes on time. It always does.

"Did he just stop coming?"

"Well he married again and moved out of the city. He and his wife had a baby, a boy."

"That must have been hard for you," Maya said.

"It was. I didn't want to act weird or anything."

"Let me tell you. Whether your father knows it or not, there's no finer boy than you, that's for sure."

"Thanks." Andrew smiled. "Well it got harder for him to come. My mother was pleased. She didn't have to deal with him. At Christmas and our birthdays, he shows up with expensive presents and my mother says, 'What a waste of money. It should be used for their college funds.' He still calls once in a while. I find with parents it's just easier to tell them what they want to hear. You know? Like I'm getting all A's, playing baseball and plan on becoming president. My mother keeps saying we don't need him. She's wrong. I do need him and Ally does too." Andrew had never said this out loud. It felt good to tell Maya.

"Why don't you tell her that, and your dad, too?"

"I don't know. Maybe someday. We better get going. What else do you want to show me?"

"My church. My grandmother goes every Sunday."

"Your church? Didn't you ever hear of cutting and going to the mall."

"The mall is not a special place for me. I'm not into expensive things."

They walked a couple of blocks before Andrew could see the steeple with the cross on top and a bell tower underneath. When they got to the big wooden doors, Maya asked, "Do you pray, Andrew?"

"Sort of," he answered.

"It doesn't matter. You can come in anyway."

Maya led Andrew down the side aisle of the darkened, empty church. Andrew admired the rainbow-colored stained glass windows around the church. Maya stopped in front of a rack of small red candles. She whispered to him, "Hold my hand. I am going to light a candle for us. It's a very special way of praying." She lit one candle in the first row with a thin wooden stick. Then she bowed her head for a few seconds and squeezed Andrew's hand as the little light flickered inside the red glass.

"Andrew, I'm glad no one is here but us and God."

"How do you know God's here?"

"I know. Believe me."

"Maya, you always surprise me," said Andrew.

"I already told you the last surprise, *mi casa*."

"Are you sure it's safe?" Andrew asked as they left the church and walked toward the house.

"No, Brainiac. But, I want you to see where I live. I grew up in the apartment building around the corner. But a few years ago, my brother had one of the old houses knocked down to build this." She pointed to the beige stucco house.

"Sure is big compared to the other houses on the block," said Andrew.

"That's my brother. He has to have the biggest and the best in the neighborhood."

When Maya opened the front door with a security code, they stepped into a large marble hallway. Off to the right was a living room with two large white leather couches and glass tables.

"We never sit in there."

"Why not?"

"Too fancy, my *abuelita* says. Expensive things don't make a family. Here's where we spend most of our time, in the kitchen." Maya was already into the large fridge, putting bowls on the stone counter top.

"Do you like Mexican food?" she asked.

"Does Tex Mex count?"

"I am serving you my *abuelita's* famous enchilada stuffed with chilies, onions, and avocado." He enjoyed watching her prepare the meal. Just as they started eating the delicious food, he heard a noise and looked through the kitchen window. The Mustang was pulling into the driveway.

"Maya, someone's coming."

"Quick, hide," she yelled, pushing him toward the door to the basement.

He ran down the stairs, and started groping along the wall for a light switch. He heard a dog growling and saw its brown eyes glistening. Suddenly a huge black German Shepherd rushed toward him, barking and snarling.

Andrew turned a door knob and stepped into the black space of a closet filled with boxes. Somehow he managed to shut the door before the dog got him. The dog growled and jumped up against the door. Andrew held the knob tight from the inside, scared to death of the dog and of Cruz. He could hear the conversation above him in the kitchen.

Maya called, "Shut up, Diesel," but the barking dog continued scratching at the door of the closet. Andrew thought, Diesel, what kind of dog is named Diesel? Not a boy's best friend type of dog. That's for sure. He could hear Steely talking in the kitchen.

"What are you doing home this early? Why is that damn dog barking in the basement? Let me guess. You are your brother's sister, always walking a thin line. I think your brother's not here. I hope not, for your sake. Don't forget to tell him I came by."

"I won't," said Maya.

Andrew heard the door close and then her steps rushing down the basement stairs while she was yelling at the dog in Spanish.

I should have paid more attention in Spanish class, he thought. The dog had stopped barking but Andrew could still hear it growling. Outside the closet door, Maya called, "Dost thou love me?"

"Are you for real? Call the dog off, Maya."

With that she opened the door. As soon as Andrew stepped out, Diesel knocked Andrew right off his feet.

"Get him off me," Andrew screamed.

Giving another command in Spanish, Maya grabbed the dog by the neck and put him in the garage.

"This isn't funny, Maya."

Laughing, she said, "I didn't know Diesel was down there. Just because he has been trained to eat any boy who has kissed me, you don't like him?"

"Let's get out of here, Maya. It's not safe."

"Andrew, turn around. See my brother's snake tank against the back wall? The reptiles only strangle boys who hold my hand.

We didn't hold hands inside the house, did we? But, maybe they know anyway. Snakes are like that."

"I am out of here," said Andrew, zipping his jacket.

Maya walked Andrew to the train station. She said, "You know, Andrew, you still haven't answered my question. "Dost thou love me?"

"I must be nuts. Considering you fed me to a dog named Diesel and I still love you, Maya. You are my loco girl."

"I love you too, Brainiac. You make me think. Not to mention how cute you are."

Andrew wanted to kiss her right there. But remembering this was Cruz's neighborhood, he didn't. Would he ever get over his fear of kissing her?

Maya said, "Listen Andrew, I hope Ally has a good game tonight. I tried to explain to my brother how important it is for you to be there but he doesn't care."

"Whatever," Andrew lied. He didn't want Maya to be upset, so he avoided going into how much he wanted to be at that game tonight. He just said, "Be happy. I had fun with you today."

On the train ride home, he thought, You could learn a lot about a person from hanging out in her neighborhood. Walking from the train to his house he was thinking how close Maya lived but how different her neighborhood and world were. From the street Andrew could see his front door was open and his mother was looking out.

CHAPTER 6

"Well, Andrew, obviously you now need an electronic bracelet so I can trace your every move. The dean called to tell me you not only cut classes but left school for the entire day. He apologized for having to call me with this information on the day of Ally's big game. It's sad that the dean feels bad, but my own son could care less how much he hurts me, especially on such the day of Ally's showcase game."

"Mom, I didn't deliberately hurt you. I just can't stand being locked in like this."

"Where were you today and who were you with? I want to know right now."

"No, you don't," he shouted as he ran upstairs to his bedroom and slammed the door shut.

"Well, I hope you enjoyed slamming your bedroom door for the last time, because tomorrow I am having that door removed. Then you'll start to know how jail feels."

Andrew lay on his bed, staring at the ceiling, wondering how he was ever going to get to the gas station to meet Steely or tell Ally that he wouldn't be at her game.

He got up and knocked on Ally's bedroom door.

"Can I come in?"

"Sure," Ally replied.

He said, "Hey hotshot, ready to kick some serious ass tonight? I know you can. I have major renovation plans for your bedroom next year when you're off living in one of those fancy dorms reserved for super jocks."

"Really, Andrew? Because I heard mom is ordering bars for your bedroom windows. Do you need all this attention from her? I'm afraid to ask you what you have been up to."

"Ally, I'm in trouble with that guy Cruz. I'm supposed to help him tonight. How am I ever going to get out of here and back in time for your game?"

"Andrew, you can't go there tonight. You know my friend Carolyn's father is a cop? She heard him say that the DEA will be waiting to bust Cruz at the el tonight."

"What, you knew this and you're just telling me now? Quick give me your phone. I have to warn Maya."

First Andrew phoned Maya. No answer. He left a message: cops are ready to move in on your brother tonight at the el. Then he texted the message and waited for a reply. When there was none, he said, "No word from Maya. Something's wrong. Maya always answers my calls and texts. I have to go warn her now."

"You can't go. Think about Mom," said Ally.

"I can't let Maya get arrested."

"Cruz's guys don't play. They'll hurt you or worse."

"I gotta go, Ally. I can stop this."

"I'm going with you. I'll drive you."

"No, you're not. Tonight is your big game. You worked your whole life for this."

"Do you think I could play knowing you were there with them? If we hurry, we can be back in plenty of time for me to get ready. Come on, we're wasting time."

Andrew grabbed his jacket from his room. As they ran down the stairs, Ally called to their mom, who was cooking in the kitchen. "Mom, I forgot to get a card and a thank-you gift for the coach. We're just running down to the drug store. We'll be right back."

"You don't have time for that now, Ally." When their mom saw

Andrew leaving with Ally, she started screaming, "You've got to be kidding. Andrew, come back here now."

"We'll be right back. Promise, mom," Ally answered. They ran to the black Honda. Ally backed out of the driveway, watching their mom running after the car.

They headed toward Cruz's neighborhood in rush hour traffic. Ally had a heavy foot, weaving in and out of traffic wherever possible. All of a sudden Andrew spotted the red Mustang heading toward the el in the opposite direction.

"That's them. Turn around." Andrew yelled.

Immediately Ally made a U –turn, moving closer and closer to the car. The Mustang was two cars ahead of them, about to turn left, when the light changed.

Andrew yelled, "Floor it."

As they moved into the intersection, out of nowhere a tan sedan came straight toward their black Honda. The red Mustang continued on its way. Right before they crashed, Andrew realized what was about to happen. The only thing he could do was to put his hands up to protect his face. He heard Ally scream and felt the pain of the airbag bursting into his chest as the sedan slammed into them. Their car swerved across the lanes. Brakes screeched and horns blared. When he looked up at the shattered front windshield, he thought Ally had gone through the glass, but she was still strapped in the seat belt. She was writhing in pain saying, "My leg, my leg!"

A guy on the street yelled, "Don't move. We called 911."

Andrew could already hear the sirens growing louder. Like a dream, cops appeared and started asking him questions about what had happened. He stammered out answers, watching Ally moaning with tears running down her cheeks.

Two ambulances came. EMT's were stabilizing Ally's leg on a stretcher. When they asked Andrew if he was experiencing pain, he said his wrists hurt. They were both swollen and red. The EMT thought his wrists might be sprained. He then examined Andrew's face cleaning and bandaging the cut near his right eye.

"What happened to the guy who hit us?" Andrew asked.

"He went to the hospital, the EMT said. "Looked like minor cuts and bruises."

One of the cops was on the phone with Andrew's mother telling her that they were taking them to Shoreview Hospital. The ride in the ambulance was surreal. The driver kept cursing saying drivers didn't move quickly enough to the side to let the ambulance pass. Ally couldn't talk, just sobbed softly on her stretcher.

When they wheeled him into the emergency room, his mother rushed over to the gurney. "Andrew, Andrew are you all right?" She gently touched his cheek.

It was strange, but Andrew never remembered his mom being so happy to see him.

"Yeah, Mom, it's my wrists that really hurt. What about Ally?"

"She's in X- ray now. They think her right leg is broken."

"O God, no! She missed her game tonight all because of me. Now her leg is broken. Oh, God, I'm so sorry."

"Listen, Andrew, you both could have been killed. You're alive. We have to take care of your injuries now."

His mom kept running back and forth between the room where Ally was waiting for the results of the X-ray and the hallway where Andrew lay on a gurney.

Finally, a young doctor wearing wire glasses examined Andrew. He said that Andrew's facial cuts and bruises were superficial. There were chest bruises from the impact of the airbag, and both his wrists were sprained from when he covered his face. They sent Andrew for X-rays but, as the doctor had predicted, he had no serious internal injuries.

The doctor said, "I'm releasing you. Make sure you ice your wrists when you get home. See your private physician tomorrow. I can see you work out. Take it easy for a while."

Work out, Andrew thought. I'll never be able to go the gym again and face Cruz after what happened tonight. He wondered where Cruz and Maya were now. Had they been busted? Were they at the police station? It was all such a mess.

Outside in the hallway to the emergency room, Andrew heard his mother talking to an orthopedic surgeon. Ally's break would require surgery in the morning. His mother stood so erect and spoke so calmly and efficiently. Andrew's eyes filled up with tears. He wished he could relive tonight and stay home. Then Ally would be at her game, not in this hospital facing surgery. Quickly he blinked away the tears. He didn't want his mother to see him crying.

Andrew was happy to get into the cab with his mother and leave the hospital.

But he felt so guilty leaving Ally still there.

"What about the damage to the car?" Andrew asked his mom.

"We can always get another car. I could never replace you or Ally."

His mother was acting so different. Just replace a $ 20,000 car. No lecture, no loan he had to repay with his first job.

When they got home, his mother threw her coat on the living room chair and ordered a pizza with garlic knots. Not her usual salad and grilled vegetables. She fixed the couch with pillows and blankets for Andrew to lie and rest. She got him ice packs for his wrist. Then she put on boxing for him. He didn't even know she knew he liked boxing. Next she went inside and returned his phone and iPod. "I'll put your TV back in your room tomorrow."

Andrew was in shock. It was like his mother had been in the accident and hit her head.

"Andrew, are you comfortable? I have to go inside and make a few phone calls."

"Yeah, Mom. Thanks for everything."

"Yell if you need anything."

As soon as she left, he phoned Maya. She answered immediately. "Oh, Andrew, I heard about the accident from some of the guys on the street. Are you all right?" she asked.

"Are you all right, Maya?"

"Yes, yes. First tell me about the accident."

"I sprained my wrists. Other than that, just minor cuts and bruises. But Ally busted her leg on the night of her big game."

"I'm so sorry, Andrew. Tell her I hope she's better soon."

"Actually, we were driving to the el to warn you about the DEA bust. Did the cops bust you?"

"Yes, Steely got arrested."

"What about your brother?"

"No, for now he's safe. Actually he's the brains behind the deals. He rarely goes to the sales. He doesn't even do drugs or drink or smoke."

"Are you kidding me?"

"No, everyone is surprised to hear that. He says why would he poison himself like that?"

"I tried calling and texting you to warn you about the bust."

"My brother won't let me answer my phone when a deal is going down. When can we see each other again? I've been so worried."

"I don't know. I can't leave my mom now. Ally is having surgery in the morning. I got to stick around for her and my mom. This is all my fault."

"But, Andrew…"

"Listen Maya, I can't see you now. My mom's coming back in. I'll call you after Ally's operation."

When Andrew's mother returned, she sat in the big wing chair near the couch.

He couldn't remember the last time she watched TV with him.

"Are you okay, Mom?"

"It's just I keep thinking that I could have lost you and Ally in this accident."

"You didn't. I'm here and Ally is going to get better. You know, Mom, I can understand that you're upset about Ally. She didn't deserve any of this, especially on the night of her big game. But, to tell you the truth," he swallowed and went on. "I'm surprised that you feel so bad that I'm hurt. The accident was my fault. You and Ally told me not to get involved with Cruz. Ally was taking me to see him, so I could warn him about a drug bust."

His mother's eyes widened, but all she said was, "Andrew, let's not go there now. First you and your sister have to get better."

"Mom, you treated me so nice tonight."

"What are you saying, Andrew, that I don't treat you well? The last few days you have been punished, and rightfully so."

"I'm not talking about being grounded. I'm just saying I know that I'm your son and that you love me. Sometimes I think you don't even like me."

"What are you talking about, don't like you?"

"I mean a lot of time you put down guys."

"Men in general, not you, Andrew."

"Mom, in case you haven't noticed, I am a guy. Sometimes you act like you know how guys feel. But you know, you never ask me how I feel about stuff."

"Andrew, is this about dad?"

"No, Mom it's about me."

"But, I know you miss him. Don't you?"

"Yeah, I do."

"I feel bad about that. We couldn't stay married. We grew in different ways. I needed more from my career. He didn't understand. I tried to make up for him not being here. No matter how hard I try, I can't be two parents."

"I don't want you to be him."

"What do you want, Andrew?"

"Well sometimes I'd just like you to admit he exists. Did you even tell him about Ally's accident?"

"Yes, I called his attorney and left all the medical information and the doctors' phone numbers."

"Mom, didn't you want to talk to him and tell him what happened? And tell him how I didn't mean for it to happen?"

Suddenly Andrew started to cry. He didn't want his mother to see him cry. Crying always made her uncomfortable.

His mother got up from the chair and started picking up the dishes and her shoes and coat. "Andrew, we've have had a very difficult day, and now, with Ally in the hospital facing surgery, I think the best thing for us to do is to get a good night's sleep. I am going to bed. If you need me during the night, just call."

Trying to control his crying, Andrew said, "I want to watch some more TV. I'll see you in the morning."

"Don't stay up too late," his mom said.

Andrew watched her go inside her bedroom and close the door behind her. He hadn't meant to talk about how she hated men. The words just spilled out of his mouth. He especially regretted bringing up the subject of his dad.

When he turned off the TV, he decided to sleep on the couch. At midnight came Maya's text, "A thousand times good night." No, not a good night. Tonight was horrible. From the couch, he could see the bright moonlight pouring through the kitchen window. Andrew couldn't sleep. He kept worrying about Ally, Cruz, Maya and even his mother. About the consequences hanging in the stars - the consequences of his own gigantic mistake.

CHAPTER 7

Andrew had no idea what time he actually fell asleep. When he awoke, the bright sunlight told him he had overslept. It was past noon, and Ally's surgery had been scheduled for seven. His mother had gone alone. He got up, dressed, and grabbed a banana. No sense calling his mom. He knew she would tell him not to come. When his mother faced problems, she usually pushed everyone away, like handling difficulties alone proved her strength and independence.

But Andrew didn't want her to be alone. He needed to help her, if he could. His wrists still were sore. Instead of riding his bike, he took the train and walked a few short blocks to the hospital. The attendant at the front desk told him Ally was in the recovery room.

Just walking through the hospital hallway made Andrew claustrophobic. The heat was stifling. He breathed through his mouth to lessen the smell. He consciously looked forward to avoid seeing the half-naked patients lying in their beds. The thought of Ally trapped here because of him made him feel sick. What could he possible say to her? When he got to the recovery room, he could see his mother by Ally's bed. Her leg was raised.

Andrew finally caught his mother's eye and waved for her to come into the hallway. Stepping outside the room, she whispered, "Come in, Andrew. Ally is still groggy, but she's awake."

"I can't, not now. I don't know what to say. How did the operation go?"

"The surgeon says it was successful. We have to wait and see how it heals. You're sure you won't come in?"

"Maybe tomorrow. I just wanted to make sure she was okay. I'll wait for you in the lobby."

"I might be a while. Why don't you go home and get some rest? Thanks for coming."

"No problem. See you at home."

At home the phone never stopped ringing. Friends, coaches, teachers saying how sorry they were and hoping Ally would heal quickly. Andrew thought, They're sorry and they weren't even responsible for what happened. Near dinner time, Max arrived with trays of food.

"Wow, there's a lot of food here. Tell your mom thanks."

"In good times and in bad my mother cooks. So start eating. She's cooking more as we speak. It sucks about your sister. Will she be okay?"

"How could she be? Her soccer scholarship will be gone. All because of her idiot brother."

"What happened?" Max asked.

"Well, you know I'm involved with Maya. Ally found out that the police were going to bust her brother. We were rushing to warn them when we were hit by another car. It was totally my fault."

Andrew could see Max couldn't handle this, so he added, "How about we play a little X Box. I feel maybe you'll let me win today."

"Fat chance."

They sat side by side, fingers flying, minds focused. Andrew did feel a little better, even though Max destroyed him game after game. When his mother came home, Andrew asked, "Did the doctors say when she can play soccer again?

I asked the doctor that very question. He said, "Let's first focus on getting her walking again."

The next day Ally had been moved to a room filled with

giggling girlfriends, flowers, and balloons. Andrew squeezed into the room. When he kissed her on the forehead, Ally hardly looked at him. When he hugged her, she held her body stiffly, the way their mother usually responded to hugs.

With all her girlfriends in the room, there was no pressure to keep a conversation going. Finally he said, "I'm shoving off. I'll see you tomorrow."

Ally replied, "I'll be here. That's for sure."

Going down on the elevator he wished Ally had screamed at him that she hated him for doing this to her, instead of being polite. Then it would be out in the open. Keeping all these feeling inside was like waiting for a volcano waiting to erupt.

The next day Andrew returned to school. He could tell the way the kids looked quickly into his eyes, then down at the floor, that they felt sorry for him. With both his wrists sprained, he couldn't participate in gym. While he was sitting on the bleachers, suddenly Ski walked into the gym and motioned for Andrew to follow him onto the track. Ski caught the gym teacher's eye; the other teacher nodded.

"Since you're just taking up space on the bleachers, I thought a walk in the fresh air might help. I hear you had a rough ride the last few days. So you want to tell me about it?"

"The doctor said Ally would be released by the end of the week." Suddenly the words poured out. Andrew told Ski how he and Ally got into the crash trying to warn Cruz, and how Ally would probably hate him for the rest of his life. "She's not even talking to me. None of this would have happened if it wasn't for me." Suddenly Andrew's eyes filled up with tears. "I'm sorry, man," he said to Ski.

"No need to be. It's okay to feel sad. You have a lot to be sad about," Ski said, putting his hand on Andrew's shoulder.

"These days all I do is say I'm sorry to Ally and to my mom."

"How is that working for you?"

"Sorry never worked much in our house. You know, when I was little and said I was sorry after making a mistake, my mother would say, 'What good is sorry?' "

"What do you think about that?" Ski asked.

"Well, I think sometimes being sorry isn't enough. Maybe now I should try to do something to help my family."

"Like what?" Ski asked.

"Well, I have to stop seeing Maya. I feel like being with her is betraying my family. My mother and sister want me to break away from Cruz."

"Have you explained this to Maya and her brother?"

"No. Maya keeps texting and calling. I just can't face her. I miss her so much, but I know I have to stop seeing her. Her brother--nobody can talk to him."

"Do you think that it's fair to Maya, avoiding her?"

"Of course not. But part of me doesn't want to break up with her. I think about her all the time."

"When do you think you should talk Maya about this?"

"Soon."

"What about your mom? How are the two of you getting along?"

"Well, it's worse now that my mom is trying to be nice to me. I don't know what to do. The terrible thing is that when she eased up on me and gave me back my phone and privileges, I really hurt her."

"How did you do that?"

"I told her that I missed my father."

"How did your mom react to that?"

"Well she went into her bedroom and closed the door. When she shuts the door on you, it's airtight, like a tomb. What's worse is facing Ally. She is coming home but her soccer scholarship and dream of an Ivy League school is gone. Her own brother in the next bedroom is responsible for it."

Ski paused and said," Andrew it's not as if you made the other car hit yours."

"No, but Ally wouldn't have been in the car if she wasn't helping me."

"Andrew, give her some time. Ally isn't just a great athlete. She's intelligent and sensitive, like her brother. From what you told me about your relationship before the accident, you love each other a lot. Love like that doesn't just disappear because you made a mistake, even a serious one. Give Ally some time and space.

In the meantime, what are you doing for yourself?"

"What?"

"When will you be cleared to work out again?"

"I go to the doctor's next week."

"Well, find out when you can start exercising again. It will help ease the tension. You worked so hard to build some muscle. You don't want to lose that now."

"Yeah, you're right, I guess."

"Listen, good luck with Ally coming home tomorrow. Tell her I hope she's better soon. We can meet here the same time on Friday if you want."

"Okay. We'll meet out here."

"If you need to talk to me before Friday, contact me on the school website."

"Thanks."

"No problem."

Walking back to class, Andrew thought, talking to Ski really helped. Ski just listened without judging him. That was a new feeling to talk like that to an adult for Andrew. It felt great.

Ski was right. He had to be honest with Maya. Andrew texted her to meet him in the stairwell at lunch time. When he saw her waiting there for him, she looked so beautiful, he almost lost his courage.

He had hoped they could go into their old hideout, the storage closet, and talk, but Maya had other plans. "Oh Andrew, I miss you so much. Let's get out of here now."

"Cut, now? No, Maya, I can't cut anymore. My mom is having a rough time. I can't cause any more problems for her. That's why I haven't called you or texted you. My family doesn't want me involved with your brother. How can I see you and not him? I think we just have to cool it for a while."

Maya started screaming, "You are breaking up with me in the hallway? You're such a little shit. Everyone told me that. I didn't want to listen. I told you that we would have to fight your mother and my brother to stay together, and you promised. Remember? I should have never believed you. You are so weak. You couldn't fight a cockroach."

Maya was yelling so loud, a crowd was building around them. Andrew said, "Calm down, Maya." He went to put his arm around her.

She started crying hysterically, "Don't touch me. You don't deserve to touch me. You're pathetic."

Now some of the guys from the handball court gathered around Maya. Ray said, "Is this slime bothering you?"

Before Maya could even answer, Ray punched Andrew in the face. Andrew tried to grab Ray's neck. Within seconds, Ray's handball partners had Andrew on the floor and were kicking him. The kids started to crowd into the stairwell, chanting, "Fight, fight." Andrew felt punches land all over his body. As the deans and teachers were yelling to move aside, the boys stopped beating Andrew and started to slip into the crowd. Right before the deans got to Andrew, Ray spat in his face and then ran.

In the dean's office, Andrew begged them not to call his mother. But school policy required that a parent be contacted immediately when a student was involved in a physical confrontation. No matter how many times the deans asked him, Andrew said, "I don't know the guys who jumped me and I have no idea why." The deans tried to get kids who were there to tell them what happened. No one saw anything.

His mother sat silently in the office as the dean recounted the incident. When they asked her if she knew about Andrew's involvement with Maya Cruz, she simply said, "Yes."

When they left school, his mom called their family doctor to check Andrew out, especially his wrists. In the car ride to the doctor's, his mom asked, "Andrew, this fight today has to do with Cruz and his sister. Doesn't it?"

"Yeah, Mom. It was because I'm trying to get way from them. Please believe me. I tried to break up with Maya. She started crying and her friends jumped me."

"Do we need to call the police?"

"The police? Uh-uh, you don't want to get involved with Cruz and the police."

"Should I make an appointment with the principal? You could transfer to another school if you want."

"No, I can handle it." He didn't know if he really could, but he didn't want his mother involved now.

"Andrew, why are you getting in all this trouble? Do you need more attention? It has to do with Ally, doesn't it? Ally has been so successful. She's gotten more attention, more praise."

"No, Ally is great. She's always been great. The funny thing is I know a lot of times she's embarrassed or feels bad for me about the attention she gets. Look what she sacrificed for me now. I just hope she can forgive me and we can go back to the way we used to be."

"Andrew, we can't go back. You know that. If this trouble you've gotten yourself into isn't about Ally, is it about your father? The other night you said you miss him."

"Mom, you're panicking, coming up with solutions that don't make any sense. Dad doesn't know anything about Cruz or Maya. How could he fix this any better that you? The truth is I have to work on it myself. Today some jerk just started a fight. That's what these kids do, fight all day long."

"Why did you ever get involved with these kind of kids? They're dangerous." His mother shook her head.

"First of all, they're not all like the idiot who started the fight today. Like I tried to tell you before, Maya is really smart and funny and feisty. She just has to fight to get what she wants. Actually, you and she have a lot in common, though you wouldn't think so at first."

"I don't understand, Andrew. You had such nice friends, like Max."

"Sometimes I just get bored and want to meet different people, go to new neighborhoods."

"I worked so hard to pay for you and Ally to live in our neighborhood."

"I know that, and I appreciate it. I just want to know what else is out there." He was silent.

"What else - like selling drugs? Andrew, what kind of choice is that?" Andrew was silent. "So now it's out in the open. Selling drugs is what you were doing in the park the last few weeks."

Andrew sighed, "I wasn't exactly selling drugs. I never touched them. But yeah, I helped him. That's why we were going to warn Cruz. I didn't want to hurt you."

"Really, it's seems to me that selling drugs is all about hurting. Of course, I'm hurt. Who wants their child involved with drugs? What about the other people you hurt? The kids who buy them, their parents? What's going to become of these kids? Andrew, I know you don't want to involve the police. But I know it was that Cruz gang that beat you up inside your own school. You're lucky that you're not in jail with a record now. Soon you might not have a choice about involving the police."

"Listen Mom, I wasn't involved that much. I'm working on getting out of this, I swear. I think it's already over as far as I'm concerned. How did you know anyway? Did Ally tell you?"

"She told your father, who has visited her several times in the hospital."

"Nice if I knew that. Don't you think, Mom?"

"Well, if you feel left out by your father, don't. Actually he'll be at the hospital lobby waiting to see you."

"Now ?"

"Yes. I'm going to drop you off right after Dr. Hartwick checks out your wrists."

"What am I going to say to Dad?"

"Frankly, I don't know."

Andrew was nervous. Walking into the waiting room, he could see his father reading the newspaper. Probably the sports section, Andrew thought. His father loved sports. His dad was heavier than he remembered, and now he was wearing a goatee.

When Andrew called, "Dad," his father jumped up and kind of leaned forward toward him and put his arm around Andrew's neck. His father showed affection so much more easily than his mom. Then his dad said, "Let me have a look at you. I hear you were roughed up in school today. Are you okay?"

"Yeah, yeah some little jerk just started a fight. Nothing I can't handle. I told Mom."

"You put on some muscle. You look stronger."

"Thanks, Dad."

They sat across from each other kind of awkwardly.

"I'm sorry, Andrew, we haven't seen each other more. I've been so busy. A baby certainly keeps you up all night."

"It's all right," Andrew said. As he was saying this, he knew it wasn't all right. He didn't know why he was letting his father off the hook. He never let his mom off the hook.

His father said, "I hear you've been in a lot of trouble. You want to fill your old man in?"

"From what Mom says you know most of it from Ally now anyway."

"She didn't want to tell me, Andrew."

"You would have found out anyway. I'm pretty sure I'm out of it now. Today I told Maya I don't want to see her or her brother anymore. Since the big police bust I haven't seen or heard from Cruz."

"You know, Andrew, if you're in a jam, you can call me anytime. I'm not that far away. I feel terrible about Ally's broken leg."

"She's coming home tomorrow." Andrew said,

"I know. Like I told Ally, I'm sorry, but I can't be here tomorrow to help get her home. My schedule is too tight."

"We'll manage," said Andrew.

"I feel bad about everything. Ally is depressed. As far as helping her with college tuition, I can't do it. I'm buried in credit card debt now with the new baby and paying child support for you guys. Now you're hooking up with these low life kids, Andrew.

Maybe, it would help if I was around more to kick your ass now and then. But I'm sure your mother does that on a regular basis."

"She's tough, but it hasn't been easy for Mom. That's for sure."

"Your mother doesn't believe in easy. That I know from experience. Listen, I got to hit the road. The traffic at this hour is brutal. I'm going to call you and your sister and set up some regular visits again. How does that sound?"

"Good."

"Maybe we can catch a ballgame or two?"

Baseball was his dad's sport. Andrew found it kind of slow and wasn't that much of a fan. His father hugged him and said, "Listen, keep your nose clean. If things get worse with these kids, maybe I can help you. I wish I could say you could come live me, Andrew, but Heather is kind of funny that way. With the baby and everything, there's not much room."

"I don't need to live with you. Like I told Mom, I can handle this. I can take care of myself."

"Now you sound just like your mother. Take it easy. We'll be in touch."

Andrew didn't reply, but he thought, I'm not like Mom. Maybe I'm like Dad. Maya had said that Andrew was afraid to fight for what he wanted. His father didn't seem to be able to fight for his own kids. Why didn't his father have the guts to tell his wife that he needed to be a father to his first set of kids? Why had his father just let Andrew's mother push him out of their lives? Maybe he was a coward. Maybe they both were.

CHAPTER 8

Andrew could feel the heat of his tears inside his eyes as his father slowly walked out of the hospital. He saw his mother quickly walking toward him carrying Ally's bags.

"Dad left? I can see it didn't go well between you."

"Meeting with Ally here in the hospital and me in trouble at school isn't exactly a party."

"Well, Andrew, your father has difficulty facing problems. That's part of the reason I had to take charge when we were married. If I hadn't, where would we be now? You know Andrew, I don't hate all men, just ones that act like idiots. The most important thing is now life is fairer for girls like Ally than it was when I was her age."

"Even with a broken leg and no money for college?"

"Let's hope so. First she has to get back up and start walking. I think her cast will be on for about six more weeks. Then hopefully she'll start physical therapy. I feel confident she'll do well with that. She's used to exercise and is very disciplined. As far as college for her, I've started researching on the Internet. There is scholarship money available for bright girls like Ally without sports. If she doesn't get that, she'll have to consider the state schools with lower tuition. I haven't talked to her about this yet. She'll have to face it sooner rather than later."

"Has she told you, Mom, how she feels about what happened--

the accident and how she was trying to protect me? Did she tell you it was all my fault?"

"When she describes the accident, she just says that you and she were in the car together. She hasn't even talked about missing the showcase game. No, Andrew, she hasn't been blaming you. Listen, I'm going to need you tomorrow to come with me to help get Ally with her cast in the car and upstairs to her bedroom. I don't know how agile she is on the crutches yet."

"Sure, Mom. No problem."

Andrew still hadn't given Ally a get-well gift. Something that would make them feel closer. Then he thought of Curious George, the best gift she had ever given him. When he was really little, Andrew loved Curious George. The little stuffed monkey went everywhere with him. Then one day in around the third grade, Andrew came home to find Curious George gone. When he asked his mom if she'd seen George, she simply said, "You hardly ever play with that anymore, so I donated it to the Salvation Army toy drive. They will sell it and give the money to poor families."

With Curious George gone, Andrew cried himself to sleep while his mother said, "You are being ridiculous. You're getting too old for stuffed animals now." But the next day when he came home from school, Ally was standing at his bedroom door. "Someone is waiting for you in your room," she said. When Andrew opened his bedroom door, Curious George was sitting on his bed. Ally had taken money out of her piggy bank and gotten her friend's mother to take her down to the Salvation Army Store and buy back the little stuffed monkey.

He knew exactly where he had hidden George. In the storage bin George was looking a little old and faded, but Andrew shook him out, stuck a welcome home sign on his chest, and sat him on Ally's bed.

Then he texted Max to come over with the music for their *Romeo and Juliet* song. The portfolio projects were due soon. With the accident and Ally's surgery, they hadn't been able to practice much.

Max brought over his keyboard and played a deep, loud refrain.

"Is this angry enough for the dying Mercutio?"

"Yeah," Andrew replied. "We'll use that for the hook, 'a plague o' both your houses!'" Andrew told Max they needed a wilder sound for the words "scratch a man to death."

Max played a few different high notes. Then he came up with a combination that Andrew liked. Andrew had highlighted words in the speech that were needed to tell the story. For about an hour they tried to match sounds with the words.

Finally Andrew said, "We've done enough for today. Your homework, Max, is to come up with a gory sound for the words, "worms' meat," the dish that Mercutio will turn into when he's dead."

"I'll get right on it," Max said, rolling his eyes.

"Our song is sounding fine. Don't sweat it, Max. I won't be in school tomorrow. Ally is coming home."

"That's great," said Max. "Tell her I hope she's better soon."

The next morning Andrew could tell his mother was anxious to get Ally home without any difficulty. She had brought home all Ally's things the night before so they just had to concentrate on getting Ally into the house.

When they arrived at the hospital Ally was up and ready to go. Seeing her dressed and out of bed, Andrew thought she looked so small. The hospital attendant took her to their car in a wheelchair. They were quiet on the drive home. Getting into their house wasn't easy. But going up the living room stairs to the bedroom was the most challenging.

"Maybe Andrew could just carry you?" his mother suggested.

"No," Ally responded.

When her crutch slipped off the third step, Andrew tried to hold her up.

"Don't touch me," she said. She was turning toward Andrew when she lost her balance and fell down the stairs.

Crying, she lay at the bottom of the stairs. Andrew felt terrible, seeing her helpless.

He said, "Ally, I was just trying to help."

"Stay away from me. I don't want your help."

"Andrew, let me handle this," his mother said.

Without a coat Andrew ran out of the house. He just started running. He found himself going in the direction of the park. From the sidewalk he could see the empty swings where he and Maya once sat being pushed by wind. He could hear the handball being smacked against the wall. Moving side to side, her long black hair swaying, Maya was in the game again. He couldn't tell who she was playing against.

Andrew checked his cell phone: 1:20 PM. Maya was cutting. He had a sudden urge to call her on his cell and yell at her. He didn't call because of the guys with her. The last thing he needed was another beating.

On the way home Andrew started worrying about Maya's English assignments. The final test on *Romeo and Juliet* was next week. He wondered what she thought about how the play ended. She was probably angry at Romeo for giving in so fast and drinking that poison. And what about Juliet stabbing herself?

With Maya you never could guess. He didn't get it. Why did she refuse to speak in class when she knew the answers? She said school wasn't for her. Yet she had really gotten into *Romeo and Juliet*. She must have saved 100 quotes from the play in her phone. She had even shown Andrew sketches for her portfolio project, where she drew illustrations that would accompany the quotes. She drew very well. Just because they broke up, she shouldn't cut class and hurt herself. She'd worked too hard to slip back now.

He looked back at the handball court. The game was breaking up, Maya and most of the guys left through the front gate. He noticed Ray running up the hill by himself, slipping through a hole in the back fence. Just seeing Ray made Andrew angry. Andrew wondered why he was leaving the park alone and going in a different direction. He remembered Maya saying she knew shit about him that her brother didn't even know.

So Andrew found himself following Ray. Of course, he stayed far behind, hiding behind the trees. Andrew watched Ray stand off to the side of the sidewalk until a silver Lexus pulled up. The driver was a blond, skinny girl around eighteen. Ray jumped in to the passenger seat where they exchanged goods; the girl clearly giving Ray a wad of cash.

Definitely Cruz didn't back this transaction. Cruz would never trust an idiot like Ray to do business at all. Cruz's business was never done on a busy street in broad daylight like this. Out of the car, Ray caught a glimpse of Andrew, who turned and ran as fast as he could back into the park. He almost made it to the swings when Ray caught the back of his hoodie, pulling Andrew to the ground. When Ray bent over to remove the knife from his boot, Andrew kicked Ray right in the head. Ray was dazed but still punched Andrew in the mouth. Andrew made a fist and let Ray have it right in the teeth.

"Hey, you two punks. Get out of here now. I'm calling the cops," yelled a park attendant. Both Andrew and Ray ran back out into the street through the hole in the fence. Ray's mouth was bleeding and Andrew felt sore around his eyes and cheekbones. His wrist was killing him, but Ray definitely had taken a beating.

"You're dead when Cruz hears about this, Junior," Ray yelled.

"Yeah, well, you better tell Cruz soon, because if he finds out what you are up to, you won't be telling anybody anything. That's for sure."

Andrew promised himself that he wouldn't contact Maya anymore. But, he just had to tell her about how he got back at Ray. He knew she would be proud. He texted her about the fight in the park: Ray didn't like that I saw him doing some business on the side. Fight, gave him a bloody mouth.

She replied, *"Magnifico.* That slime had it coming. If he even thinks of coming near me, you'll see the scars."

By the time Andrew got home, Ally's posse of giggling girls were entertaining her. Actually Andrew enjoyed hearing Ally laugh again. He snuck into the downstairs bathroom to assess the damage to his face. His face was already bruised from being jumped in the stairwell, but today's cuts and bruises were stinging. Aside from his wrist hurting like hell from punching Ray, his lip was swollen. Since his mother had an eye for microscopic detail, he knew he better come up with a reason for his most recent bruises. Even though his body ached, Andrew felt good. He knew Ray hadn't expected him to fight back. He made an ice pack for his lip and slipped quietly into his bedroom.

He had hoped Ally would eat with them tonight to distract his mother. But she ate dinner in her room, saying she wanted to catch up on her school assignments.

As soon as they sat down to eat, his mother asked, "What happened to your face? If those bruises have anything to do with those thugs you hang around with, we should call the police now."

"I'm okay, Mom, really."

"We've been to the emergency room once already this year. Don't you think that's enough, Andrew?"

"Really, Mom, everything is going to get better soon. I got it under control now."

His mom just looked at him for explanations and answers he couldn't give her —not tonight, anyway.

He wished he could tell Ally about the fight with Ray. He missed talking with her.

He gave a quick knock and opened her door to see her typing on her lap top at rapid speed. He knew the teachers told her to take her time but Ally plunged right into the assignments. Once she started working, her concentration was amazing. She could have written a research paper in a packed football stadium and not heard any noise.

She didn't look up, but Andrew noticed Curious George sitting on the pillow close to her.

"I just wanted to say goodnight," Andrew said.

"Don't the freshman get homework any more?"

"I'm saving it up to see if I can do the work for a whole marking period in one night, like my sister does."

"No, you would need my special powers to do that."

Andrew was so relieved. At least Ally was talking to him.

"I wanted to tell you. I moved my stuff out of the bathroom up here. You can have it all to yourself."

"You don't want the cripple to make you late for your workout in the morning. Is that it?"

"No, that's not it, Ally. I just wanted to make things easier for you."

"Haven't you done enough?"

That was the first reference Ally had made to Andrew causing the accident.

"Listen, Ally, I've tried to tell you a million times how sorry I am, but you won't let me. What do you want me to do? Tattoo I'm sorry across my forehead?"

"That's an idea," she said.

Slamming her door shut, he went to bed and pulled the covers up over his head. He had messed up that chance to talk about the accident. He wanted to talk to her so much. Why had he snapped at her like that? Ally had a right to have an attitude. What did he expect? He wanted her to forgive him so much. Now she was home but was acting so different. He missed the way she used to be.

At breakfast his mother asked, "Do you think slamming your sister's door is the best way to fix your relationship, Andrew?"

"Truthfully, Mom, I don't know what Ally wants me to do. She just pushes me away no matter what I try."

"She is just hurting now. You better get ready for school, Andrew."

"Yeah, I don't want to be late. Today the *Romeo and Juliet* portfolio is due.

I have to make sure I have got our project ready to go."

At school Andrew ached to see Maya. He was late to three

of his classes because he lingered by her classroom door, hoping to catch a glimpse of her or even maybe start a conversation. Andrew counted on meeting her in the library, where all Ski's English classes were setting up their portfolios. On his way to the library, he passed her on the crowded staircase. Usually when that happened, especially now that they had broken up, she would become louder and crazier. A show that she could do just fine without him. As she walked past him, Andrew was shocked to see her looking pale, tired and sad. She just looked away to avoid eye contact with Andrew. He called to her, but she didn't answer.

He started to phone her on his cell when Max punched him in the shoulder, "Today is show time. Mercutio, are you ready to die in a musical way?"

"Ready and dying to curse both families," Andrew answered.

Ski had set up the front of the library as a performance area. A couple of students were re-enacting the famous death scenes. Students in the roles of Romeo and Juliet were drinking poison and stabbing themselves. Many performed the scenes using the original text. Others rewrote the ending, like having the young lovers run off to escape the prejudice of their families.

As they were watching the performances, Andrew whispered to Max, "I'm ready. I got the words memorized."

"Not to worry, because the audience will be listening only to the music."

Right before their performance, Ski whispered in Andrew's ear, "I know your song is about fighting. Your face was banged up enough. You didn't have to do any more damage to it."

Andrew kind of smiled and said, "You should see the other guy."

"Really?" Ski said.

"Come on Andrew, I have the keyboard ready."

"Okay, relax, Max."

Max started to play. Andrew heard the introduction and started spitting out the story line. He played Mercutio who had just been stabbed by Tybalt. Andrew yelled out, "I am hurt." He leaned over as in great pain and quickly transitioned to the refrain, "A plague o' both your houses."

The kids in the class were getting quiet, a sign they were listening and really getting into it. Andrew went on to sing about Tybalt, the expert swordsman. Tybalt's sword scratched Mercutio to death. As the music swelled, Andrew held his side, and cried out to the class, "Ask for me tomorrow, and you shall find me a grave man."

In approval the class joined in on the final refrain, "A plague o' both your houses."

Andrew was glad that it was over. He thought they didn't do too badly. But Max just rolled his eyes and said, "Do you think we'll be starting a band any time soon?"

"Definitely." Andrew answered. "We'll call it Around the Corner."

Max socked him in the arm and asked, "Are you going to come around or are you still in love with that hot pepper?"

"Don't call her that."

"Touchy, touchy."

"I am, Max. Maya and I broke up. With her brother in trouble and my mother pressuring me, it just got too messy. But, I miss her a lot."

"Oh," Max said, "Hey, I'm sorry." Andrew nodded.

Long tables in the back of the library displayed all kind of projects. Some girls had designed a model village of Verona, complete with Juliet's balcony. There were lots of drawings inspired by the original play. Andrew was just about to leave the library when his eye caught the midnight blue canvas covered with stars tucked away in the corner. In bright red letters was Romeo's quote, "I fear too early, for my mind misgives Some consequence yet hanging in the stars." As Andrew looked closely at the canvas he saw a sleek silver airplane flying through the starlight. In green letters the word *HOPE* was painted on the side of the airplane. The artist's signature, Maya, stood out in the lower corner.

He wanted to tell Maya how awesome her final project looked. But he just couldn't bring himself to call.

CHAPTER 9

Andrew's mother was still driving him to school every morning. The next day she had the talk radio station on in the car. Andrew tuned out a story about a guy found murdered until he heard the name: Ray Garcia, a student at John Glenn High School. He had been found dead under the train trestle late last night. His throat had been cut.

Andrew could barely swallow. Ray, who he had just punched out in the park, was now dead – murdered, with his throat slashed. The radio announcer said that Ray had alleged connections to a local drug dealer.

"Andrew, is this about the boy you have all the trouble with, that Cruz? You want me to take you home?"

"No, Mom. He's not going to hurt me. God, Ally got hurt because I was trying to help him. I have no idea how or why Ray was killed." Andrew lied; he thought about what he had seen at the park, Ray's double dealing in the Lexus. And, he'd told Maya about it. And, Maya must have decided it was time to tell Cruz—not just because Ray was cheating Cruz, but to protect him from Ray. And Cruz had killed Ray.

Oh God, he thought. What if the police knew he and Ray had been fighting in the park?

There were police all over the front of the school. They had set up a scanner where all the students had to be checked to see if they were carrying weapons.

He went across the street and texted Maya, "Ray's dead. Cops everywhere. Scanners at the front entrance." Immediately she replied, "Don't sweat it. Ditched the knife last night." Last night, Andrew thought. My God, why last night? Because she knew what her brother was going to do. Or was it her brother? He didn't want to think about that.

Most of the students entering the building had never been searched, and were very upset, going through the invasive process. Some of them were crying. The principal was in front of the building, reassuring parents that the building was safe and counselors were being brought in if students needed to talk. Talk? Andrew thought. That was the quickest way of losing your life. Of course, Maya was nowhere in sight. And today was the final on *Romeo and Juliet*.

The essay question on the test asked: What did you learn from reading *Romeo and Juliet*? The fighting was what had interested Andrew the most in the play. But he wrote his essay on this test about love. Andrew described how love changed Romeo and Juliet. At first they thought of each other as enemies. In love they discovered the best in each other. Then they had to decide whether or not to follow the lifestyle society dictated. Andrew wrote, "Though Romeo and Juliet were unsuccessful in changing their lives, Shakespeare shows us that love can empower us to live differently."

When he handed in his test, Ski asked him if he was okay. Andrew nodded; he wanted to lay low with the murder investigation in progress. Going home, Andrew thought about life like dominoes, one event triggering a toppling of the other dominoes that couldn't be stopped. He kept looking over his shoulder for Maya or the police. What would happen now that Ray had been killed? Who would take the fall for Ray's death?

As the days passed, the excitement over Ray's death diminished. The police had swarmed all over Cruz and the guys who worked with him. But, according to the news, no witnesses or hard evidence was found. Still, every night Andrew expected a knock at the door.

He could envision them interviewing him at the dining room table with his mother looking on. When he tried calling Maya, a recorded message said that the number was no longer in service.

No one, not even Ski, knew what was going on with her at home. Ski said the only official information was a phone call from her grandmother indicating Maya was ill and wouldn't be in school.

After a week without news of Maya, Andrew was frantic. Then, late one afternoon, the red Mustang pulled up next to the curb where Andrew was walking. Andrew was surprised to see Cruz alone in the car. He had almost expected to see Ray sitting shotgun.

Cruz rolled down the passenger side window. "Get in," he barked. "Where is she?" Andrew had never seen Cruz angrier.

"Maya?"

"No, your mother."

"I haven't heard from her in a week, I swear. She hasn't been in school or phoned or texted me."

"I know all about that. Today she took all her shit and ran away. My grandmother is crazy with worry. Since this morning I have my guys looking everywhere. *Nada.* Now it's getting dark. She's fourteen. My sister alone on these streets. Just think about the bottom crawlers on the Ave. finding her. Not to mention the slime at the depot. Where can she be? Think."

"I don't know. A couple of weeks ago, she took me to some places where she hangs out by herself."

"Take me there, now," Cruz said. Andrew hesitated. Then he opened the car door and climbed in.

First, Andrew told him to drive to Maya's elementary school. The look on Cruz's face when Andrew showed him the field in back of the school was disbelief.

"You gotta be shitting me. This is where she likes to go?"

When they got to the church, Andrew thought Cruz would break his ankle trying to kick the door in.

"She's not in there if it's locked," Andrew said.

"This is all you got?"

'Well there's one more place, I'm not sure," Andrew said.

"What are we waiting for? A team from the morgue to find her? Where to?"

"The airport."

"Would they sell her a ticket? Where the hell would she go?" Cruz thought out loud. Andrew could see Cruz was livid. He was silent on the way to the airport. They drove from terminal to terminal. Finally in one deserted waiting room with her nose pressed up against a window, she stood there watching a plane taxiing down the runway.

"Maya," Andrew called. She turned, happy to hear his voice. When she saw her brother, she bolted. Within seconds, Cruz grabbed her arm and twisted it as she screamed.

"Scream out again," and he said something quickly in Spanish. She immediately stopped yelling as he pushed her to the exit and the parking lot.

"Maya, Maya, it's going to be okay," Andrew called to her. They were several yards ahead of him. As they got closer to the car, Andrew saw Cruz start to beat Maya. He slammed his fist into her face and shoulders and head. She had her hands up, protecting her head and face.

Running toward them, Andrew yelled, "Stop it, you, bastard, you'll kill her!"

By the time he got up close, Maya was on the ground and Cruz was slapping her face. Andrew grabbed Cruz's arm to stop him. Cruz turned, pushing Andrew away. Maya was on her feet starting to run.

Cruz yelled, "Son of a bitch" and grabbed Maya. When she threw herself on the ground, he dragged her by the hair back to the car. Then he opened the door and shoved her into the backseat.

Cruz turned toward Andrew, pointing a small black revolver right at him. "Don't put your nose in other people's shit."

Andrew stood speechless in the parking lot while the Mustang peeled away.

He walked back to the terminal and then took two buses to get back home. He had left a vague message for his mom that he was involved in a school project and wouldn't be home for a couple of hours. He knew she wouldn't believe it, but that was the least of his problems.

Andrew couldn't even think about what Cruz might do to Maya when he got her home. How could Andrew protect her? He knew he couldn't call the police. He couldn't tell his mother, who would call the police. If he told Ski, he would be obligated to report the abuse to Social Services, and Maya could end up in a foster home. She loved her grandmother so much. Andrew just couldn't do that to her.

Finally, he got off a bus that left him on the Ave. He found himself in the back parking lot by The Pit, where Cruz hung out. He could hear guys playing pool. But after a few minutes of waiting, he saw a brand new white Cadillac Escalade pull into the lot and out stepped Steely.

Andrew had heard he got out of jail. The new hot car was a bonus from Cruz, no doubt. What exactly had Steely done to earn it? Taken the fall at the drug bust?

As Steely made his way to the back door, Andrew called his name.

"What the hell are you doing here?" Steely asked.

"I just came from helping Cruz find Maya."

"So what do you want--a medal?"

"The thing is, he was beating her really badly."

"In my opinion, she needs roughing up. If she stopped flapping her mouth and started wiggling her ass more, she would do a lot better."

"I mean, he was hurting her. If someone doesn't stop him, I think he might kill her."

"Okay, so you told me. You done your civic duty. Now go home and say your prayers."

Disgusted, Andrew turned and walked down the Ave. When he finally got home, he was trying to figure out an excuse that might calm his mother. But when he opened the front door, he found his father sitting in the living room talking to Ally. She was resting with her leg up in the recliner. The empty pizza boxes indicated that he had missed dinner.

Oh, jeeze, he thought. I forgot.

His father said, "Well it's about time. Where you been, Andrew? We waited, but the pizza was getting cold."

"That's okay. I had to take care of something for school."

"You sure it didn't involve beer or pot in a parking lot?"

Andrew got nervous when his dad mentioned a parking lot.

"No, Dad, I wasn't drinking or smoking."

"Well you weren't in the library, that's for sure. Never mind, you're home now. Ally and I are talking about some things the three of us might do together as a family. What do you think, buddy?"

Buddy, his father hadn't called him that in years. Andrew had almost forgotten that name.

"I don't know. I'm kind of beat. It's been a long day."

"No time to let your Dad in on how your life is going? I want to know."

Andrew wondered, How much did his father really want to know? Did he want to hear about Cruz selling drugs and beating on Maya, who Andrew loved and couldn't protect? Did he want to know Ray was dead? Then there was his mom, who had trouble with him being a guy, and let's not forget Ally, whose college dreams he had destroyed. Exactly where was he supposed to begin, and how much family time did his father have before he had to rush back to his wife and new son? Andrew knew he clearly couldn't tell his father any of this. He wondered if he ever would. But to satisfy his Dad's fatherly conscience, Andrew went through the litany of assignments and activities he was involved in school.

Finally his dad said, "Well, it sounds like you are keeping busy. Okay, you two talk it over and come up with some places where we can go and have some family fun. I'll call Ally in a few days and we can set a date."

"Sure, Dad."

"Goodnight, sweetheart," he said to Ally, kissing her on the forehead. "You take care of that leg now."

When he left, Andrew and Ally just looked at each other.

"Where's Mom?" Andrew asked.

Ally replied, "She vacated so we could have Dad time. It would have been nice if you showed up on time."

Andrew said, "I forgot. I just got a lot on my mind. I'll try harder next week. Now I'm exhausted. I'll see you in the morning."

Ally replied, "Tomorrow is my first day back in school."

"I'll help you any way I can. You know, freshman bro, carry your books and be your personal slave."

"Sounds tempting," she said. "The school is issuing me an elevator pass and letting me leave classes early to avoid the crowd in the hallway. They're even giving me a second set of books so I don't have to carry too much. Tonight Dad brought me an iPad, the Internet at my fingertips."

"Cool-- you deserve it, Ally."

"Thanks, Andrew. See you in the morning."

This was the first normal conversation he'd had with Ally since the car accident. Andrew was grateful. At least it was a start. Before the accident he could have told Ally about what happened at the airport, but not now. Andrew wished he knew where to turn to help Maya.

Lying in bed, he remembered Maya asking him if he prayed. Tonight he prayed for Maya's safety. Maya wasn't in school for the next couple of days. Ski was pressuring Andrew to meet with him, but Andrew was afraid. What would happen to Maya if he told Ski or any adult about Cruz beating up Maya? Then again, what had happened to her because of his silence? Steely clearly wasn't interested in defending her. Maybe Steely knowing made it worse for Maya. A rule of the street was "Snitches get stitches." Cruz wouldn't like Andrew telling Steely about the beating at the airport. Andrew hoped Cruz didn't take it out on Maya. Not knowing was the worst.

It was good to have Ally back in school. Andrew shadowed her in case she needed help maneuvering through the halls. Actually he was more of "gofer" for Ally's friends. The only one who didn't want him to do anything was Ally.

Andrew had really never thought Ally was like their mother before. But under stress Ally was a lot like her. She worked intensely to be independent and to stay active. Andrew thought, maybe I'm not like Mom or Dad. But I could be more like Ally if I tried harder.

That Sunday was Halloween. Max and he always went trick or treating. Max said, "Hey, I'm game if you are. Think of the candy."

Andrew said, "No, I think I'll pass." He helped his mom give out treats to the neighborhood kids. Actually, he and his mom had fun and laughed a lot.

The following Monday, during first period, Max sent Andrew a text: Maya is back. Anxiously waiting outside her classroom, he barely recognized her. Her long black hair had been cut. It barely covered her ears.

But he hugged her right there. "Thank God you're alive. I was so worried."

She smiled and hugged him. "Meet me this afternoon after school in the park by the swings."

His mom still demanded that he come home straight from school. But Andrew didn't care. He had to be with Maya now. Andrew ran all the way to the park. She was sitting on a bench. He sat down next to her and put his arm around her.

"Oh, Maya, I thought your brother was going to kill you for sure when I left you in that parking lot. Your hair--did he do this to you? "

"No, I did it to spite him. Do I look ugly this way?"

"Maya, you would be beautiful without hair. Tell me what happened."

"The real trouble started when Ray was killed and the police swarmed our house. It was really hard on my grandmother. The cops were trailing my brother twenty-four-seven. He started getting paranoid, throwing away my phone, not letting me see anyone, making me stay inside the house. With you gone from my life, I had no one who understood. I just couldn't take it any more. So I decided to run away."

"I would have never taken your brother to the airport if I had known he would hurt you like that. He seemed so upset that you were out alone on the street. Like he really cared."

"With him the beatings are about power. When we came home from the airport, my grandmother was crying, yelling, 'Maya, *mi bebita*, I thought you were dead in the streets'."

My brother screamed, "She'll be better off dead when I get through with her. Running away like that."

"I ran into the bathroom and locked the door. I was looking in the drawers for something like a razor to defend myself. I found scissors. When I looked in the mirror at my hair and thought of how he dragged me by my hair across the parking lot, I got so angry I cut all my hair off. I was thinking, he will never pull me by the hair again."

Andrew nodded, letting her talk.

"With my grandmother screaming in the background, my brother kicked in the bathroom door. When he saw all my hair over the bathroom sink and floor, he went berserk slapping me. 'You want to see cutting. I will show you cutting.' He threw the scissors against the wall and took his knife from out of his pocket and flicked the open blade up against my face so close that little droplets of blood ran down my cheek. I was too scared to move. Then he whispered, 'You try a stunt like this again and I'll show you how cutting is done, not your hair but your face.'"

"I could still hear my grandmother crying in the kitchen. My grandmother is a very gentle, peaceful woman. She never raises her voice. She prays every day. When my brother beats me, she always begs him to stop, but he never does. She usually goes into the kitchen and cries while he's hitting me. This time she came out of the kitchen with his gun and said to him in Spanish, 'Enough.

Touch her again and I will kill you.' My brother could have taken the gun from her easily. But I think he was so shocked. We never heard her even curse at us. He started yelling, 'You let her get away with this. You'll see what happens.' He threw the knife on the ground and stormed out of the house and drove away."

Andrew held Maya tight and let her keep talking. "After he left, my grandmother was crying hysterically. She couldn't even look at the gun. I put it back in his dresser. My grandmother said, 'Maya, we have to leave this house. We can't live like this no more. It is not safe to live here. Your brother will not change. Tomorrow I will call your uncles in Arizona and see if we can go live with them."

Andrew, with his arms wrapped around her said, "Let me see. Even though weeks had passed, he could see black and blue marks around Maya's eyes. Andrew gently kissed her face. "I should be able to protect you. I feel so bad I can't."

"No one can. My brother is crazy. My grandmother is right; he won't change. That's why we are going to move."

"You're really going to move away? When?"

"Soon," Maya answered.

Andrew felt so sad, he couldn't speak.

Maya said, "I just took the make-up test for *Romeo and Juliet*. You know that question, What did you learn from the play? I wanted to write I knew the ending would be sad for me and Andrew."

"Maya, you know we had to break up. After the accident, my sister's leg was broken, and her scholarship chances were gone because of me. She wouldn't have been in that car accident if I hadn't been involved with your brother. So, I had to stop helping him. I wish that I could end it with your brother and still see you, but you know that just wouldn't work, not now. He wouldn't allow it."

Maya said, "Families can be a bitch. So like Romeo and Juliet, we can't be together because of our families?"

Andrew paused, "Well, at least we're not dead like Romeo and Juliet.

Maya, tell me you didn't really write about us breaking up on the *Romeo and Juliet* test, did you?"

"No, you know what I learned reading *Romeo and Juliet*? I learned that words are awesome. That is why I have over 100 quotes from the play stored in my phone. And that's what I wrote about. Flipping open her phone, Maya started reading them aloud: "A pair of star-crossed lovers take their life," "My only love sprung from my only hate," "These violent delights have violent ends," "My love as deep. The more I give to thee the more I have, for both are infinite." It's not just about what I learned, but how I learned to say it."

"Wow," Andrew said.

"I promise in my new school I will be the brainiac. And you know what else, Andrew? I want you to know I will never forget how you tried to protect me from my brother in the parking lot."

"I asked Steely to help you that night. Did he ever come over or call?"

"He's too afraid of my brother to do that."

"I guess moving away, flying away, is the only way you will be safe. I saw your project in the library about the consequences in the stars and the plane called *Hope* flying there. Really cool, Maya."

"Well, me and my grandmother won't be riding any slow-ass donkey. We will be taking that plane out to Arizona."

"Did your grandmother get the tickets already?"

"Yeah and I'm going to get another book by Shakespeare to read on the plane. I've been rereading *Romeo and Juliet*. I came to the part where Romeo is banished and Juliet says goodbye. I thought of us. I have it saved in my quotes on my phone."

"You're still writing them down? The test is over, Maya."

"Shut up and listen, Brainiac. Romeo is banished and Juliet asks Romeo 'O, think'st thou we shall ever meet again?' Romeo answers, 'I doubt it not; All these woes will serve for sweet discourses in our times to come.'"

"So what does all that mean, Maya?"

"Someday you will take that plane called *Hope* and fly out to Arizona and see how gorgeous and smart I've become. Then all our sadness will be history. We'll just hang out, maybe in the stars. Who knows? So I'll be watching the skies for you to come."

"Is this goodbye? What about school tomorrow?"

"I'm out of here, Brainiac. No sense dragging it out. We'll text each other."

"Before bedtime. Right?" Andrew asked.

"Whenever, Andrew, I don't know how often I can call. My uncles are kind of strict. Don't get me wrong. They aren't crazy, like my brother, but I know they won't want me calling boys from there."

"Maybe it's better that way. The sound of your voice would make me so sad, I'd want to put my hand through the phone and touch you. Call me when the phone can let me do that."

Without thinking Andrew grabbed Maya and kissed her so hard, she had to lean backwards to keep her balance. Tears were running down her cheeks. He was crying too, and for once he didn't feel ashamed.

"Listen, Maya on the count of three, we'll just go in opposite directions. So neither of us has to watch the other leave. You count, Maya, I like the way the numbers sound in Spanish."

"*Uno, dos, tres,*" Maya called out.

From the sound of her voice, he could tell she was crying. He wanted to turn and wipe the tears from her cheeks. Instead he ran as fast as he could. He didn't turn to look back, but he did look up at the sky.

CHAPTER 10

For Andrew it was like Maya died that moment they left each other in the park. Every cell in his body seemed to shrink. His chest tightened so, when he realized he wouldn't see her today or tomorrow, or the next day. Who knew if they would ever see each other again? At first he didn't tell anyone. To say the words out loud was too painful.

He tried to resume the life he had before he met Cruz or Maya. He felt like an imposter. At home he helped out his mom and tried to be especially nice to Ally. Twice in one week, he rode over to the Ave to get her sushi. He attended classes and completed the homework. He even went to the weekly meeting of Notes. It seemed as if every song was about breakups and broken hearts.

The silence was the worst part. No phone calls, no texts, no sound of her voice in the stairwell, no glimpse of Maya in the hallways between classes or on the handball court. Sometimes he thought he saw her on the swing, but he knew she wasn't there.

Ski was the first person to reach out to him. Ski sent Andrew an e-mail saying, Maya Cruz has been taken off my class roster, transferred to Arizona. If you want to talk, see you after 9th period.

After school they walked out to the field together. The cold November wind made Andrew zip his hoodie while Ski turned up the collar of his jacket. The best thing about Ski was the way he listened. Andrew knew he could say as much or as little about

Maya as he wanted. He didn't tell Ski about the airport, or Maya being saved from Cruz by her grandmother. It was safer not to tell anyone about that.

Ski asked, "How are you surviving without Maya?"

Andrew said, "Just about making it through each day. I can't tell you how much I miss her. He swallowed, and burst out, "I just can't believe I'll will never see her again."

"Is never the right word, Andrew?" Ski asked.

"Well sure, when we split, we softened it with maybe and someday. But, that's so far away. I need to see her now. Tomorrow is too far away."

"Do me a favor, Andrew. Just get through today."

Andrew answered, "I'm trying. You know what the craziest thing of it all is? We both knew that breaking up was the only thing to do. With Maya's brother, my mother, and Ally's broken leg, we just couldn't be together. Not now. It's better with Maya in Arizona. I can't see her. If she was still here, I'd always be tempted."

"Right decisions can be painful. How about your family- - how are things going?"

"Well, there's tension for sure, but at least we're all trying. My mom has really reached out to me. I'm surprised that she's been so open to my dad's visits."

"You wanted your dad back in your life. Now that you see him, is that helping you?"

"Well, it's weird. I missed him so much. Now that he's back, like a weekend kind of Dad, I kind of resent him."

"Why are you annoyed?"

"All the time he wasn't there. Now he thinks can just walk right back in. He really doesn't know anything about what I've been doing. I just tell him the stuff he wants to hear."

"Why is that?"

"Truthfully, I don't think he could handle what really happened."

"Who couldn't handle this --you or him? Maybe he already

knows more than you think. Why not try being a little more honest and see what happens? He may just surprise you."

"Maybe."

"What about Ally?"

"She's super organized and into physical therapy big time and busy researching college funding. We talk, but it's not the same. Honestly, I don't think she'll ever forgive me."

"Let me ask you, Andrew, let's say somewhere in the future Ally does forgive you. Do you think you could ever forgive yourself?"

"I don't know. I never thought about that."

"Well it's something to consider. Andrew, finally, the question I ask every time we talk. Have you hit the gym yet? It's way past time you did."

"Nah, I just haven't been up for it yet," Andrew lied.

Leaving the field, Andrew thought how he really longed to get back to the gym. But, he was terrified of seeing Cruz. Watching Cruz beat Maya had been so terrible that he had to help her. Meeting Cruz now, in an everyday place like the gym, was totally different. It scared Andrew, even more since he had gone against Cruz.

He biked from school to the Donner's house. It didn't matter what he and Max did. Andrew was comfortable sitting next to him while Max stared at some kind of screen. They didn't even have to talk. Andrew needed to visit today. But when he got there, the kitchen was dark. Mrs. Donner wasn't home, but Max, half awake, came to the side door.

"Hey, Andrew, come on in."

"Your mom's out?"

"Everyday. She got a job with a catering service. College fund needs big time help. "How do you like that?"

"Well, the food isn't as good. I like having the house to myself."

"I just felt like coming over, you know what I mean?"

"Sure, Andrew. We go way back. The other day in science someone mentioned skunks, I started laughing thinking about the time we went camping with my parents. Remember, you and I were walking on the pitch black road and that family of skunks surrounded us and we didn't know what to do?"

"I remember, and we started screaming for help until your dad heard us and came with his flashlight and got us."

"Maybe it's not so good we got each other's back if all we can do is scream," said Max.

"That's only if we get in trouble in the real world. If I have any problems in cyberspace, my friend, Max can fix it as fast as a thumb flexing."

They sat and talked, but Max didn't mention Maya. Andrew couldn't figure out why not. Surely Max had noticed that she wasn't in his English class anymore.

Andrew let it go. Maybe Max was just trying to go back to the way things were before he ever got involved with Cruz. But Andrew knew today he and Max had a good conversation and their friendship was still alive. They were watching a replay of a favorite boxing match when Andrew's phone rang. He thought it might be Maya, but no, it was his Dad who rarely called him on his cell.

"Andrew, it's Dad. What are you doing this Sunday?"

Andrew's mind went blank. He replied, "Nothing I can think of."

"I already cleared it with the general. Mom doesn't have you scheduled for Sunday. I got two great seats to the football game. Me and you will go and make a day of it. I'll make my famous four cheeses, three meats and all the toppings I can fit on a hero. Plus, buckets of hot chocolate to keep us warm. What do you say?"

"Sure, Dad."

"Dress warmly. I'll pick you up at 11AM."

"See you then."

When he got home, he noticed his mother's car in the driveway, but the house was quiet. Then he remembered Ally was at physical therapy. Last week she had her cast removed and had started rehab. Unlike his mother's prediction, she hated it. PT for an athlete of

Ally's caliber was a bore. But, Ally, like a disciplined soldier able to follow instructions to a tee, went faithfully to therapy and practiced non stop at home. Andrew would be in a conversation with her and notice her squeezing her thigh muscle while they were talking. She was fanatical about getting back into shape.

"Mom?" he called.

"I'm here in the living room reading. Usually I pick up Ally from PT now, but Carolyn is going to drop her off today."

His mom looked so comfortable, curled up with her book. Andrew felt happy to see her relaxed for a change.

"Did your Dad call you?" she asked.

"Yes, he did. We're going to the game this Sunday. He said he cleared it with you first."

"I thought you would enjoy the game. Andrew, you've been looking kind of down the last few weeks. Are the meetings with Dad upsetting you?"

Andrew paused before answering. Andrew knew his mom sensed the change in him after Maya left. He definitely didn't want to talk to his mom about Maya moving. In the old days, he would have told Ally, but now the name Maya was a hot button. No sense going there. Andrew was just grateful that Ally was talking to him at all.

"No. It's been awhile, so Dad and I don't really know each other anymore. But he's trying."

His mother sighed. "You got it right when you said that your dad is attempting to make things better now. That has to count for something. It's funny, Andrew, that you say your dad doesn't know you. I always thought it would be me who would have trouble knowing you. I've been giving a lot of thought to what you said the other night about me not liking men and taking that out on you. When you said it, I knew you were right. I never meant to hurt you. She gazed off in the distance, and Andrew waited for her to talk again. "Right from the start I wanted to be the best mom. I remember when you were born, the doctor yelled out, 'What a boy we have here.' Hearing I had a son scared me. I kept thinking,

How will I know what to teach you? It was so different when Ally was born. I knew exactly what I wanted to tell her."

Andrew looked at his mom. He finally said, "You know, Mom, understanding men isn't that difficult. We're not that different from you. Where we are different, just ask and then listen."

His mom said nothing. Andrew thought, Maybe she's starting to listen.

"Mom," Andrew said, urgently, "The way I've been kind of quiet? Maya moved away to Tucson. It's good. She's safe from her crazy brother now. It just kind of sucks."

His mother nodded. "I'm sorry," she said quietly.

Ally opened the door, home from PT. "Hey, little bro, did you give your geeky friend, Max, my phone number?"

"Yes," he said "Max thought he could help you find scholarship money on the Internet."

"Well, today Max texted me that he would be willing to do just that. I replied saying the Guidance office, Mom, and I have already been doing that, but any info he has would be appreciated. I said that I already know I qualify for any obscure scholarship under the heading of redheaded, yogurt eating, one-legged soccer player with a crazy brother and crazier friends." Then she smiled at Andrew in a way he hadn't seen since the accident.

When Andrew went to bed, he felt better than he had in weeks. He'd avoided texting Maya; he'd tried to make a clean break. But now he wouldn't be getting in touch with her out of loneliness. At least not so much. He decided to text her. He simply typed, "I miss you. Good night. A thousand times good night."

The next morning when he opened his laptop there in was an e-mail from Maya. She wrote:

> Brainiac, a thousand times good morning! Our trip here was awesome. Since I was seated next to the window, right after takeoff, I looked through the clouds and I saw you looking up. Flying to Arizona my airplane that I named *Hope* zoomed

through the stars. I wished upon every one for you. My uncle's house is very small, with lots of relatives speaking Spanish at the same time. You won't believe this, but nearby is a ranch with slow-ass donkeys. No one understands why I am so interested in the donkeys. I haven't found handball court yet, but I'm still looking. The girls at school have an attitude. Nothing I can't handle.

In English (the only class I pay attention) we are not reading Shakespeare, so I got Shakespeare's sonnets (that's his poetry, in case you don't know, Brainiac) from the library. I'm now not only reading them but have started writing one, called "Andrew's Song." Not one of the boys in my classes, school, town, or state are anywhere near as cute as you. I bet you're blushing now reading this. Have you seen my brother?

We have not heard from him. I'm only telling you this, but I do miss him. I know my grandmother worries about him too. It's crazy. Even though, he could have killed me when he was angry. Other times he was mad funny and generous and protective. That's the brother I miss. But I miss you most and I do still love you.

xoxo,
Maya.

Andrew wanted to reply in a way that Maya would read and reread until she memorized it. If he could only get Shakespeare to write for him. But he finally typed:

Maya,

I could never explain how happy I am to hear from you. Every day is so long without you. I avoid

111

the park and will never ride on a swing again as long as I live. As far as my routine-- same old, except nothing is fun without you. Have not seen or heard about your bro. Once in a while I do see Steely driving that fancy Cadillac on the Ave. The business under the el is still thriving from what I hear, but I spend my Friday nights with Max.

My mom is glad. She's even making an attempt to reach out to me. Ally and I continue to talk. Yesterday I saw a crack in the invisible wall between us when she smiled at me.

I'm impressed that you are not only reading Shakespeare but writing like him too. I can't wait to read my sonnet. I will keep it forever as a reminder of you. Not that I need a reminder. Maya, I still have money left over from working for your brother. I know how you feel about that money. But I would like to send it to you to buy yourself a whole library of Shakespeare's work. Please don't say no. I think that would make the money be okay. Text me your address, so I will know where to send it.

Whenever I think of you, which is always, I know you are safe and that is huge. Write when you can and when it's not too painful. Remember, Maya, we have hope and it's not just found in airplanes.

I love you soOOOOOO.

Andrew pressed the key until O's filled the page

He turned off the computer and wandered into the kitchen. He had gotten up early, and his mom and sister were nowhere in sight, so he turned on the TV and decided to fix himself a supersized bowl of cereal and watch cartoons like he used to do when he was little. But he kept thinking about Maya's e- mail. She seemed to be doing okay except for the part about missing her brother.

That made him think about Cruz. He hadn't told Maya that he still worried constantly about meeting her brother. Whenever he heard a motorcycle, Andrew panicked. He not only avoided the gym but the Ave in general in fear of running into him.

There was Maya starting a whole new life in Tucson. She wasn't afraid. I can't be either, he thought. I shouldn't be sitting here like this. I need to go work out.

He got his bag and rode his bike over to the gym. He refused to let himself look around for Cruz. It seemed funny going into the locker room, seeing some of the same people he used to see there.

Andrew stretched slowly and carefully to warm up and then he checked the weight room. When he sat down at the bench press, he placed the pin where he had left off.

He was straining and struggling to lift when the glass doors opened and Cruz walked in. Head held high, barrel chest with more tattoos added. Andrew swallowed hard. He decided even if Cruz roughed him up, he wasn't going to run away any more. Andrew stayed at the bench press, bracing himself. Cruz simply walked past him as if Andrew was invisible.

There weren't many people working out. Cruz had to have seen him. Andrew thought, What a fool I've been for not working out all this time. I let Cruz control me for so long. I don't mean anything to him now that he can't use me any more. I bet I never did.

Did anyone mean anything in Cruz's life, he wondered. What about Maya? How did Cruz feel now that she and his grandmother had left him? Did he care at all?

He added some more weight and continued working out. I have to get tough, he thought. Tough like Mom and Ally and Maya.

Tonight, he decided, he would go online and check out Shakespeare's sonnets. And before he went to sleep he would definitely look up at the stars. Maybe he'd see an airplane called *Hope*.

About the Author

Pat Gallagher Sassone (patgsassone@gmail.com), a New York City high school teacher, has known many students who struggle to make life changing choices. She is enchanted with stories in many forms such as poetry, songs, films and tweets. A graduate of Queens College and NYU, this is her first novel.